For CHERI
Hope you enjoy

INVERSION
II

CREATURES, FAIRIES, AND HAINTS, OH MY!

BY PAUL STANSBURY

First Edition
2018

Sheppard Press

Sheppard Press
461 Boone Trail
Danville, Kentucky 40422

Paul Stansbury
www.paulstansbury.com
www.facebook.com/paulstansbury

Printed in the United States of America
ISBN 978-0-9986516-5-1 paperback
ISBN 978-0-9986516-6-8 e-book

Cover Graphics by Paul Stansbury

CONTENTS

INTRODUCTION

Inversion II - Creatures, Fairies, and Haints, Oh My!, is my second volume of speculative fiction stories. I discussed my interpretation of speculative fiction, in the introduction to my first volume *Inversion - Not Your Ordinary Stories*. For your convenience, I have reproduced following this Introduction and would recommend you give it a read before diving into my stories.

In my realm of INVERSION, creatures are fictional or imaginary beings which are, as you would imagine, a bit out of the ordinary. For the most part, they are unsavory beings and best avoided. Next come the fairies: imaginary beings of supernatural powers. Usually seen in human form, they can be clever, playful, but can also prove mischievous given the right circumstances. And as for haints, those of you from the South may be familiar with the word. Haints are manifestations attributed to something beyond scientific understanding or the laws of nature - spirits and spooks so to speak. If you want to understand haints, read my first story in this collection, "Haint Blue".

As with *Inversion - Not Your Ordinary Stories,* some of these stories presented herein have been previously published, either in print or on line. I would like to express my appreciation to those editors who were willing to publish my work.

Paul Stansbury

INTRODUCTION TO INVERSION

INVERSION - NOT YOUR ORDINARY STORIES, is all about speculative fiction. From my viewpoint, this form of fiction places us in a world where the "Laws", those regularly occurring or apparently inevitable phenomenon that govern what happens to us, operate differently than what we would expect. In the speculative fiction world, the rules as we know them do not always apply. Or could it be the rules as we thought we knew them?

Speculative fiction aims to explore our world as it would be altered by posing the question "What if?" The most appealing and freeing aspect of speculative fiction is that, like the worlds it creates, it is not bound by the traditional genres of Science Fiction, Fantasy, and Horror. In fact it is not bound by any genre. It is free to adventure anywhere it likes as long as anywhere is a creation of imagination and speculation.

INVERSION means turning upside down or inside out; reversal of a normal order or relation. What better title for a collection of speculative fiction stories? When you ask "What if?", the result is not your ordinary story.

Some of these stories have been previously published, either in print or on line. I would like to express my appreciation to those editors who were willing to publish my work.

You will find in the appendix the definition of INVERGENCE, the word I invented to describe my concept of speculative fiction.

Paul Stansbury

HAINT BLUE[1]

I am of the Restless, inexorably suspended between the temporal and spiritual worlds. I belong to neither. Old Gullah women whisper our name at dusk when they warn the children not to be caught outside when the witching hour comes. "Haints! Them that's not moved on. Filled with evil and envy they is. It's mischief they desire and death they brings." It spills off their lips like a curse. They are right. Haints, you see, are not the wistful spirits longing for a last contact with loved ones still living. Nor are they wont to go about creaking floors at night to remind the living they still linger. No, haints have a more sinister purpose. I know, for I am a haint, and evil. It is my nature.

***

Sungila, my husband Jacob's Gullah nanny, told me to paint the porch ceiling blue. "Haint Blue," she said emphatically. "Gots to mix it up the old way. By hand in a pit, using milk, indigo dye and lime. An' don't forget da winder and door frames neither. Yeah, dat's what you gots to do to keep the haints away. They won't cross no water, an' the blue fools 'em. So they won't come in and get ya'." But I, in the insolence of my youth, dismissed the admonition as merely the prattling of an old women. I would not paint my home according to the prohibitions of Gullah voodoo. And so I sent Sungila away and had Jacob paint my porch white.

***

Not long thereafter the haint came for me. I did not see it, nor hear it. It just came, deep in the night, ripping away my soul. It is like tearing an unborn child from the womb, yet there remains

---

[1] "Haint Blue" appeared in Tigershark ezine (United Kingdom) # 12, 10/2016.

no visible wound to evidence what has happened. As for my flesh, instead of blood, my will to live oozed out. As for my soul, what good that had resided within evaporated like mist in the moonlight. Evil, the frozen rage of unrelenting resentment of the living, replaced it, forever corrupting my spirit.

***

As dusk descends, I see my home, long denied me by my own foolish actions. How I miss its comforts. It was nestled among the waning rice plantations. Dearest Jacob bought it for me as a wedding gift. It was a fine home, with a broad porch looking out over the Little Salkehatchie – not the tattered house it has become. We had but a short time there. How I miss my husband. He died soon after me. Where his spirit is, I do not know. I never will.

Jacob had awakened to my last dying throws. He held my lifeless body, weeping and cursing the Gullah superstitions. He could not be consoled, wailing that my death was his fault. Daddy took Jacob at his word and shot him dead at my funeral, without remorse, without regret.

After Jacob was buried and they took Daddy away, Sungila came. She dug a pit and mixed the milk, indigo dye and lime until she had just the right shade of blue. Then, she had the field hands paint the porch ceiling and the windows and doors. "Ain't no haints gonna get in here no more," she muttered, running her fingers along the blue woodwork.

***

That was long ago. The paint is now faded and peeling. I keep watch. Sinister intent makes a good sentinel. A young couple now lives in the house that was once mine. They are not from around here, unfamiliar with our history. She sits on the porch, studies her paint chart. "Banana Cream for the siding," she says to her husband, "and Extra White for the trim and porch ceiling."

"The girl at the paint store said we ought to keep the blue trim," he responds. "Said it is a Southern tradition or something like that. Something about keeping the spooks away and that the bugs don't like it." He takes the paint chart, looking through the colors. "Look here, they even got a name for it. The girl at the paint store showed me. Haint Blue."

"That's nonsense," she says tugging the paint chart out of his hands. "Who ever heard of such a stupid thing?"

She will soon find out, for I am a haint, and evil. It is my nature.

TAKERS[2]

Old Gramma Zola was the grandchild of a Shawnee medicine man. That's what she told me. And I never knew her to lie. Besides, she was so old she didn't have to lie. No one older than her lived to contradict what she said, so she could say anything without getting in trouble. My gramma on my momma's side was long dead when I was born, but Gramma's mother, Old Gramma Zola, was still living.

It was because Old Gramma Zola was the grandchild of a medicine man that she had the sight. And that's why I got it. Old Gramma was born around 1850. Nobody was sure about the exact date. Her daddy was thrown from his horse and died when she was about five. Her mama died of consumption a year or two after that. Then she had been taken in by a farmer and his wife to do hard chores. When she was fifteen, the farmer arranged for her to marry a widder-man. She said he got a pretty good price for her, and that is pretty much the story of her life. That and the fact she lived to be 103.

Old Gramma Zola was real old when I was born. Thin as a rail. I remember she spent her time mostly on the back porch in her rocking chair or in her bed listening to the radio. The back room was fixed up as her bedroom. She took her meals at the kitchen table even on Sundays when the big table was used. Always wore a faded bib apron. She had long, thick grey hair. I helped her wash it once a week. After it was dry, I would braid it into a thick cord that she draped over her left shoulder. Bright black eyes—Shawnee eyes, I suspect—looked out from deep within her

---

[2] Takers appeared in *Out Of The Cave and Other Stories*, an anthology published by Mackenzie Publishing, 2015.

wrinkled face. As I approach my ninety-sixth year on this earth, I see her face in mine when I look in the mirror.

When activities of the day had stopped and everybody readied for bed, Old Gramma smoked her pipe. She only used it when the Takers were about. She clamped it between her teeth, puffing blue smoke out from the side of her mouth. I'd plump up her pillows, and she'd pull the covers up. She kept a fan from the Robertson Funeral Home on her night stand. It had a painting of Jesus with lambs on one side and the address of the funeral home on the other. It was my job to fan her, sending the smoke drifting across the room. When it was time for me to go to bed, I would turn on the GE fan, which sat on her dresser.

On a spring night when I was thirteen, Old Gramma called for her pipe. "Takers is about tonight," she said.

"That's an old wives' tale," Momma said. "Don't be filling the chile's head with such nonsense. She don't need to be hearin' all that jus' cause you want to smoke your old pipe. She'll be havin' nightmares again."

"Ain't no tale. Your Momma didn't pay it no heed and she got took before her time. Best you start believin' and the chile, too. Well, I guess I'll go to bed so's not to upset you no more," Old Gramma said in a huff. "Can the chile come sit with me whilst I go to sleep?"

"If you promise not to fill her head with ghost stories."

"They ain't ghosts, they's Takers. There's a difference."

"I don't know, and I don't care. You been talkin' 'bout nonsense all my life an' I'm tired of it. No more talkin' 'bout Takers or you can go to bed by yourself."

"All right," Old Gramma snipped. "You won't hear no more from me tonight. Come on, chile."

6

Momma looked at me. "And you be in your bed before the clock strikes ten—or else. And don't forget to wash your face and brush your teeth."

I followed Old Gramma to the back room and turned down her covers and plumped up the pillows while she washed up and changed into her nightgown. She sat on the side of the bed, and I helped swing her legs up. She poked and prodded the pillows until she sat comfortably and then pointed to the lowboy, where her pipe, matches, tobacco, and the Robertson Funeral fan were.

I poured tobacco into the pipe and tamped it tight with my thumb before handing it to her. Clamping the stem between her teeth, she took a match and struck it along the side of the box. She waited until the flame died down before touching it to the tobacco and taking a deep draw.

"Don't like that match smell in my baccy," she said, smoke tumbling out of her mouth. "Get the fan, chile."

"Right here," I said, pulling the fan from behind my back.

"That's a good girl. Let me have that," she said, holding out her hand for the fan, "while you go see if your Momma's light is out."

I left her on the bed and made my way down the hall that led to our bedrooms. I crept toward Momma's room, careful to avoid the squeaking spots. Then I got down on my hands and knees and peeked into the space under her door. I didn't see a light. I listened a bit but didn't hear anything either, so I headed back to Old Gramma's room. She sat where I had left her, pipe smoke drifting around her head while she rhythmically moved the fan back and forth.

"Light's out," I said.

"Here, chile." She handed over the fan. "They ain't ghosts or devils or anythin' like that. They's Takers, wandering about 'til they finds someone to take away."

"You told Momma you wasn't gonna talk 'bout them no more tonight."

"Said she wouldn't hear no more from me tonight. Now that she's gone to bed and mos' likely asleep, I figure she can't hear us having a little chat."

"Ain't that lying?"

"Well, you could call it that, but I don't. Said she wouldn't hear me and she won't, so's I don't hardly think that's lying."

I thought about it for a minute. Since I had questioned whether she was lying, it'd be alright. "How d'ya know if Takers is here?"

"You see's 'em," she said.

"But you said they was Takers about tonight. I didn't see none."

She pulled the pipe from her mouth. "That's 'cause you wasn't lookin'. You can't see 'em just by havin' your eyes open. You gots to be lookin'." She pointed the stem toward the door and blew a stream of smoke in that direction. "They's one right now."

My heart pounded so hard I thought it was going to bust out of my chest.

"See for yourself."

I turned my head and looked but didn't see anything. "Don't play tricks like that."

"Weren't no trick. You think they'll let you see 'em that easy?" she said. "No, you gots to look in the shadders and the nooks and crannies to see 'em. You gots to look out of the corner of your eye to see 'em. They comes in through the key hole or slides out from behind the chifforobe. They floats up from between the floorboards and down outta the cracks in the ceiling.' An' they's just there for a second. Ain't goin' to stand around while you gawks at 'em. No, you gots to be ready. Jus' let your eyes ease out an' you'll see 'em. That's when you'll see their wisps like the

8

last breaths of morning fog hanging on the hillsides. That's what they looks like. Little bits of fog or tiny shreds of clouds that fall down toward the ground. Gone as soon as you see them. Keep movin' that fan, chile. They don't like that. Fans and smoke—no, they don't truck with that at all."

"How's that?" I asked.

"Why, chile, use your brain," she chortled. "A fan jus' blows 'em away like you would shoo a fly offen a pie with your hand. They ain't nothin' but vapors. That's why they don't like smoke. It confuses 'em."

"How they take you then?"

She spoke in a hush. "When you goes to sleep and everthin' gets calm. That's when they gets you. They come right up to your face and rides your breath inside. That's when they takes you."

I watched her lips move, hanging on every word, when I thought I saw something in the shadows by the lowboy. I must have twitched because she immediately said, "Ha! You jus' seen one—your first—but not your last. They knows you now. Don't worry none, though. It ain't you they wants tonight. Just the same, from here on out, you gots to be on the lookout. Now keep that fan goin'."

I looked around the room but didn't see anything. Neither of us said a word for some time. I jumped at every creak and groan.

"Steady, chile," she said, "they don't make noise. It's jus' this old house coolin' off and settlin' in for the night."

After a while, I got up the courage to ask, "Ain't that jus' dyin?"

"What's that, chile?"

"When they take you."

She furrowed her brow. "No, chile, dyin' is somethin' altogether different. When you dies, you goes to plead your case with God, and he sets out what you gonna do from then on. But iffin the Takers gets you, it's a whole 'nother matter. They takes you away where nobody can find you. But they leaves your body for your kin to find. That's all you need to know."

"If you goes to God when you die, where do you go when the Takers get you?"

Old Gramma squeezed up her face real tight as if she sucked on a lemon, and then said, "Well, chile, I guess you gots to know sometime. They takes you to the shadder place where nothin's the way it's supposed to be. You feels the air, but you can't breathe. You eats food, but you stays hungry. You drinks water, but your mouth stays dry. The sun shines, but you is cold. You hear the sound of voices but don't know what they's sayin'." Her voice creaked. "You sees things, but you don't know what they is. You calls out in misery, but you don't make no sound. You is thinkin' hard, but you don't understand nothin'. And you know why? I'll tell you. It's 'cause the Takers live in the shadder place and they is powerful jealous of what we got. So they come out of the shadders and the nooks and the crannies an' sucks everthin' that makes you a person right outta you. That takes a powerful long time, an' all the while you gets paler and paler until you is nothin' but a wisp and you starts wandering in the shadders lookin' for someone to take 'cause you misses it so. That's where they took my baby Susie. That's where they'll take you iffin you ain't on your guard."

That was the first and only time I saw Old Gramma cry. She didn't bawl or anything, just a tear at the corner of her eye. I didn't ask any more questions because I wasn't sure I wanted any more answers. I had enough to think on, and it weighed awful heavy on my mind. I kept fanning while she smoked her pipe.

After a while, she handed me the pipe. "Here, chile, fill this up for me."

When I had done that, she said, "Best be gettin' on to bed now before the clock chimes."

"But can't I stay a bit longer? Don't you need me to fan away the Takers?"

"Iffin you don't get to bed before your Momma told you to, that would be jus' like tellin' a lie, an' I don't put up with lyin'. You hear?"

"Yes, Ma'am," I said.

"So that's settled. 'Sides, got my GE fan to do the fannin' whilst I rests my eyes. Now jus' you turn it on and give Old Gramma a kiss before you go."

I cut the fan on. She leaned over, and I kissed her cheek.

"That's my good chile. Sleep tight an' don't forget what I told you."

I left her sitting in the bed, puffing on her pipe while the GE fan hummed on the nightstand.

The next morning, I got out of bed and went down to the kitchen. No lights were on; no coffee brewed. Momma and Old Gramma usually sat at the table sipping coffee in the morning. I went to the backroom to see if Old Gramma was still asleep. Her room was empty, too. Then I went to see if Momma was in her room. I pushed open the door and saw Old Gramma sobbing, holding Momma's hand.

She looked around at me. "She's done gone, chile. She's done gone."

I rushed over to the bed, and Old Gramma caught me up in her arms. Her chest heaved as she stroked my head with her hand. Over her shoulder, I saw Momma, her face pale and still, eyes open a slit. I buried my head in Old Gramma's shoulder and cried.

She held me for the longest time until I stopped shuddering and the tears slowed. She pulled a hanky from her pocket and dabbed around my eyes. "Chile, think you can go nex' door and

11

fetch Missus Ellis? Tell her I needs her over here. Can you do that?"

I nodded.

"That's a good chile. Now go on."

I went over and got Missus Ellis. She saw right away something was wrong. She called for the funeral home to come get Momma and helped Old Gramma with the arrangements.

No one could ever say exactly how Momma died except it was most likely from natural causes. At the funeral, the preacher said a lot of things about her going to her reward and being up in heaven and looking down on us. I knew different, but Old Gramma told me not to say anything, so I kept my mouth shut.

The Great Depression had just begun, and we had to give up the house and move in with Aunt Verda. Old Gramma died some years after that. Aunt Verda came and got me at the bomb factory one day. She said Old Gramma had been sitting on the back porch, fanning herself, and just slumped over. I was pretty sure she made it to Heaven.

***

That was a very long time ago. Nowadays, the thing about the Bell Meade Retirement Home is they won't let me smoke, but they don't care if I run the ceiling fan all night. And they say they have a backup generator in case the power goes out. Still, I keep that old Robertson Funeral Home fan on the nightstand.

Just in case.

PERCHTA[3]

Amelinda and Jurian sat by the hearth in silence. He looked at her, searching for a glimpse of the *fräulein* he had courted and married twenty years ago. Tightly braided, blonde hair, fading to white, crowned her head. Dull, grey eyes glared at him. Her lips were tightly pursed "If you believe that Perchta will come" he said, "you deceive yourself."

"Are you sure this Frau Verena is coming?" she asked, ignoring his statement. Her brusque voice betrayed her impatience. "Perhaps she has deceived you."

"No, she will come." he said, rising from his chair and stoking the fire. Standing up, he brushed back the thinning hair from his forehead. "But this would have been easier had you let me go to her and bring the wool back with me instead of insisting she bring it for your inspection."

Amelinda fixed a cold stare on her husband, a tall lanky man, slightly stooped from the constant burden of farm life. "I do not know of this Frau Verena and can ill afford another foolish decision at this time. Did you not say it was the manservant who came to you?"

"Yes, I was asking in the village where anyone could be found who had extra wool and Rolf, Frau Verena's farmhand, approached me offering a trade. He said she is a *Wohlgeboren* noblewoman who lives to the north in the Shatten Forest."

"An unusual place for a farm, I would think. And how strange that a noblewoman, even a *Wohlgeboren* of low station, would engage in barter with common folk."

---

[3] "Perchta" appeared on line in *Astounding Outpost*, 12/12/2017.

"Who can understand the follies and whims of the rich?" asked Jurian. "And what does it matter to you as long as she brings good wool? The sample Rolf showed me was of exceptional quality."

"Who are you to judge wool? If you were deceived, once in hand it could not be returned. No, if she wants to trade, then she must come and I will determine its quality."

Some time passed before they heard collar bells approaching. Jurian stood up and crossed to the window. "This must be Frau Verena's sledge. I see Rolf at the reigns."

"Go and help them," she ordered. Jurian wrapped a long woolen shawl around his neck and stepped outside.

He waited at the gate while Rolf guided the horses up to the cottage Even though he had just come from the comfort of his hearth, the bitter wind stung his ruddy cheeks. A passenger wrapped in a white cloak, face hidden by a large hood, sat beside Rolf. He pulled back on the reigns, stopping the sledge. "Welcome," Jurian said, "and thank you for coming out on such a bitter day." He could not see the passenger's face. "Is this Frau..."

"Please," said Rolf, cutting Jurian short, "a favor for an old man, fetch the *wolle* sack if you will while I help Frau Verena down. " A little gnome of a man, he nimbly hopped out of the sledge.

"Yes, of course, go on to the door," said Jurian, walking to the rear of the sledge. He peeled back the cover and slung the large burlap sack over his shoulder. He caught up with Frau Verena and Rolf as they reached the door. He pushed it open with his free hand. "Please, go inside Frau Verena, and make yourself welcome at my hearth." He still had not seen her face.

Inside, Amelinda rose from her chair, waiting as the cloaked figure walked toward her. Rolf remained just inside the door. The figure held an ebony cane which tapped on the wooden floor with each step. "Welcome, Frau Verena. Jurian says you have brought wool to trade."

"Indeed," Frau Verena replied. She drew back the hood of her cloak, revealing a finely featured face, skin the color of alabaster. Her flowing grey hair was gathered at the nape of her slender neck. She motioned for Jurian, keeping her eyes, the color of rust and gold, fixed on Amelinda. He quickly came forward, placing the *wolle* sack on the floor at her feet.

"How many?" asked Amelinda.

"Twenty fleeces," said Frau Verena, "washed and ready for the wheel."

"Like I said, it's fine wool." Jurian pulled a handful from the sack. He offered it to his wife. She took it to the window, holding it up to the light that filtered through the dingy glass.

"I'll be the judge of that," she said, rubbing the wool between her bony fingers. She brought it close to her eyes. "Average at best," she said, tossing it back to him. She turned a dour face toward Frau Verena. "Jurian says you are willing to trade the wool for five *klafters* of wood, to be cut and split before Christmas. I think you get more wood than we get wool in this trade."

"For fine wool, as your husband has acknowledged, it is a fair trade. However, if it does not suit you, Jurian can put the *wolle* sack back in the sledge and we will be off."

Amelinda scowled at the woman, then turned to Jurian, "It's your back to be traded, take it to her."

He hefted the sack on his shoulder. "Her name is Ute."

Frau Verena touched his arm, holding him still. She focused her eyes on Amelinda. "Jurian told Rolf you had brought a child into this house to do the spinning."

Amelinda stiffened. "Just an orphan from the *waisenhaus* at the Abby in Melk, brought here as a servant of this household.

15

The nuns were not sad to see her go. Most likely a *Jüdisch* mongrel, one less mouth for them to feed."

"I see, perhaps, a tainted soul in the eyes of the princes of Rome. No less tainted in your eyes by her misfortune of birth and circumstance. I shall see this child before I leave."

"Why? Who I choose to bring to this house is no concern of yours."

"That of course is true, but you shall not have the wool until I have seen the child." She turned to Rolf. "Go turn the sledge around."

Amelinda stared at the woman for a few moments, then said, "Go on, if it is your wish, but be quick about it, she has much to do and little time to do it. There will be a price to pay if her work is not finished." She nodded to Jurian.

"This way," he said, leading Frau Verena into a narrow hallway. At the end, past the regular rooms, he drew aside a rough curtain revealing a small alcove. He motioned for her to enter. Too far from the hearth for warmth to find its way there, he could see his breath as he followed her in. The cramped space was just big enough to hold a spinning wheel and a straw tick. He felt sorry for the young girl. During the summer, she had been able to venture outside the cottage to perform her chores. Then, she could at least see the sun. As winter descended, however, Amelinda confined her to this tiny room, spinning wool with only an oil lamp for light and heat. The only time she was allowed to leave it was to perform her kitchen chores.

A delicate girl with dark wavy hair looked up from her spinning as he set the *wolle* sack down. "More wool?" she asked.

"Yes, this is Frau Verena, Ute. She is a noblewoman and has asked to see you. The wool comes from her."

"Jurian, I would have a word with Ute in private," Frau Verena said.

16

"But Amelinda…" stammered Jurian, looking toward the curtain.

"I shall deal with her when the time comes. Now go," said Frau Verena. Jurian hesitated. She pointed to the curtain, "Go!" and waited until he disappeared before she moved. She reached into a pocket in her cloak, retrieving a pair of leggings. She held them out. "These are for you. They will keep you nice and warm." Ute paused, looking toward the curtain. "Don't worry about her. These cost nothing; they are a gift."

Smiling, Ute took the leggings, quickly placing them under the tick. "Thank you," she said, turning her deep brown eyes toward the floor, "but I must get back to my work. If I am not finished when Perchta comes, the mistress says I will be punished."

"Ah," she paused looking into Ute's eyes. "Perchta. What do you know of Perchta?"

"Amelinda says she is coming and if my spinning is not done when she arrives then she will be angry and I will be punished. I think maybe she is a noblewoman. Do you know her?"

"A noblewoman, perhaps. And yet there also is the Perchta of the Alpine legends. But, how would you know of those legends? The nuns at the *waisenhaus* surely would never speak of that Perchta. Not Christian enough to suit their purposes I would think. Shall I tell you?"

"Yes," said Ute.

"The legends say that during midwinter, Perchta comes in her sledge made of ice, drawn by four white wolves. She wears a crimson cloak and carries an oak branch. It is said she rewards with wealth and abundance those who have behaved well and worked hard."

Ute frowned, thinking of the *wolle* sack in front of her. "What becomes of those who don't get their work done?"

"That is a different matter altogether. Perchta deals harshly with the idle and greedy." Frau Verena lifted Ute's chin with gentle fingers and looked into her eyes. "But after all, it is but a legend. For you, Perchta will most likely be a noblewoman. Have faith my little Ute, things will be better. I have one more gift for you before I take leave," she said, reaching into the pocket of her cloak. She pulled out a small parcel wrapped in parchment. It was tied with a bit of yarn. She handed it to Ute. "Open it."

Ute placed it in her lap and untied the yarn, peeling back the paper. A broad smile appeared on her lips. Inside was a small poppy seed stollen. "Oh, thank you Frau," whispered Ute. She carefully wrapped it back up and retied the yarn. "I shall save it for later, once my work is finished."

"Good *mein kind*. Now, I am afraid I must go."

"Auf Wiedersehen Frau."

Jurian was waiting just outside the curtain when Frau Verena came out. He looked at her, but she gave no indication of what had transpired between she and Ute. She followed Jurian back down the hall and into the main room of the cottage. She stopped in front of Amelinda. "Ute says you await Perchta."

"What of it? This house has worked hard, and I am well overdue for my reward," said Amelinda.

"Perhaps you confuse Perchta with Sinterklaas, the bearded buffoon, handing out gifts from a sack. Not so for Perchta who, the legends say, spins the fates of human beings." Turning away, Frau Verena pulled up the hood of her cloak and left.

***

It was suppertime of the second day since Frau Verena's visit. Ute set the table, laying out the sausage and cabbage soup, then returned to the spinning room. Earlier, Amelinda had ordered her to set out samples of the yarn by the hearth, believing Perchta would now come that the spinning had been completed. Jurian came in with wood for the fire. He laid a log on the embers and sat down at the table with Amelinda. "Ute has finished spinning the wool that Frau Verena brought. Perhaps she could come and sit with us to take her supper."

"You are a fool to treat a foundling from the *waisenhaus*, and *Jüdisch* besides, as if she were your own flesh and blood," said Amelinda. Her brow furrowed as it always did when she was angry.

"But surely she's deserving of some small kindness. She's but a child and I had hoped that since we have no children she might…"

"Might what?" Amelinda snapped. "She is a servant, bought and paid for. She can sup on leftovers while she washes the dishes. If you desire to eat with her, take your food to the spinning room." She turned her face away from Jurian, signaling the conversation was over.

"As you would have it!" said Jurian. He went to the cupboard and retrieved another plate. "You believe that if you have worked us hard enough, Perchta will come and bestow gifts or good luck upon you. A cache of silver coins perhaps? But you do not see that in the process you have enslaved poor Ute and forsaken me. What will your Perchta think of that?"

"It is you that have forsaken me by resisting my efforts. As for the child, she is no worse off than being a slave to the nuns in the *waisenhaus*. I have been poor my entire life. Why can't I live in a fine house with servants? Why must I dig in the earth every day to eat? Why should I be poor? I have no reason to apologize for my actions."

"There is nothing wrong with working hard to improve one's status. But to gain it at the expense of others? To fail to recognize the blessings you already have and could have can only lead to woe." Stuffing some utensils in his pocket, he stacked sausage on the plates, dipped some cabbage soup in the bowl and set off down the hall.

Amelinda finished her supper. She waited for Jurian to return. As the evening wore on, the fire burned down into a small mound of coals covered in grey ash, and her mind drifted, imagining the wealth that would be hers when Perchta came.

Amelinda roused from her dreams to find Jurian had not returned to stoke the fire and it was in danger of dying. Perturbed, she rose from her chair to get some wood. She had just taken a small branch from the kindling box when, she heard the soft crunch of sledge runners in the snow followed by the panting of large animals. As she moved to the window to look, there was a sharp rap at the door.

Before she could react, the door burst open. Gusting, bitter night air swirled snow around the room. Amelinda shivered. A woman, cloaked in crimson, entered. Her face was pale as frost. Raven hair floated about her shoulders in the midwinter's wind. Her fierce eyes, the color of rust and gold, fixed on Amelinda. "I am Perchta and have come for reckoning." She struck the floor with her ebony staff. Immediately, The door behind her closed and the swirling snow fell still. The staff, long and straight twisted into a gnarled oak branch.

Amelinda studied the woman. There was something familiar in her fine, chiseled features. She gazed into the woman's fierce eyes. "I know you!" cried Amelinda. "Frau Verena? This can not be, but I fear it is. What matter of deception is this?" She looked toward the hall, ready to call for Jurian. Perchta clenched her free hand and Amelinda immediately felt fingers gently tighten around her throat.

"Leave them be. 'Tis you and I that have accounts to settle. And as for Frau Verena, I take what ever form suits my purpose, raven, grey haired noblewoman, or she who stands before you. Perhaps it is you who seeks to deceive."

"Forgive me, Perchta. I was startled and spoke foolishly. I seek not to deceive you," Amelinda pleaded. "See here,' she said pointing toward the yarn that Ute had set by the hearth. "I have laid out these samples of the handiwork of this house so you that you will recognize the work that has been performed in your honor."

Perchta looked toward the hearth. "The bounty of this house has been wrought as a result of your tyranny and not of your industry."

"Fine work, none-the-less, I think you would agree," said Amelinda. "And would it be have been accomplished had I not made it so?"

"Indeed, and as such, you believe it demands a fitting reward?"

"Yes."

"Then you shall have it."

"Praise your kindness, Perchta," said Amelinda, smiling. "And could you find it in your grace to provide some small reward for Jurian and the girl? I think it fitting they should have some small token."

"But do you not think they will see your reward as their reward?"

"Yes, of course. You are indeed wise."

"Then it is settled. Come with me," said Perchta. She waved her hand, opening the door. Amelinda followed her into the bitter night. A great sledge made of ice rested before the cottage. Four white wolves, big as draft horses, waited in the traces. They snuffled as Amelinda approached. Behind the sledge, a rabble of specters stretched into the darkness.

Perchta climbed into the sledge. She took the reigns, looking at Amelinda. Using the oak branch, she pointed to the rabble. "They are my *Perchten*," she said, "the spirits and souls whose reward is to follow me ever in the midwinter night, as so shall you." Amelinda started to protest, but her mouth filled with twigs. Perchta raised her staff. It immediately transformed into a fiery whip which she cracked over the heads of her wolves. They bolted and the sledge lunged forward into the darkness. Amelinda watched as the specters followed, churning along like so many dead leaves in a storm. As the last one passed, Amelinda was drawn in behind and disappeared into the night.

In the morning, Jurian awoke to find a fragment of a twisted oak branch on the hearth. A single set of footprints, leading from the door, disappeared in the freshly fallen snow. In the years to come, he would raise and love Ute as his own daughter, but search as he might, he never found any trace of Amelinda.

SELKIE COVE[4]

Cecelia pushed through the screen door of the Selkie Cove Inn as the cab rambled off down the gravel road, kicking up white dust. It had only taken a morning to see all there was to see in Pinniped Harbor. She had come with James on his business trip, hoping to break the monotony of their life/her life. Perhaps a spark to rekindle anything that resembled romance or adventure. She was desperate for a change—any change. A deep resentment of her drab existence had been growing inside. *What do I do now?*

The rusty return spring creaked, speaking to the building's age and condition. *Just like me.* More a bed and breakfast, the inn was simply an old house with a dining room and parlor on the first floor and three guest bedrooms on the second. The inn's saving grace was a grand view of Selkie Cove from the porch, just off the parlor. As far as Cecelia could tell, this modest concave indent in the shoreline was pristine, nothing to spoil the view, not even a tie-up for a skiff could be seen.

The innkeeper, Mrs. Merman, was a dour woman who Cecelia guessed to be in her 80's. "Find lots of pretties to buy?" the woman asked.

"Well the shops were full, to be sure," Cecelia answered, "but I only picked up some cards with a pen and ink sketch of the village. Maybe I'll go back tomorrow and find a nice souvenir to take home."

"Got plenty of postcards right here," Mrs. Merman countered, pointing to a rack of cheesy photo postcards featuring fishing boats and historic churches.

---

[4] "Selkie Cove" appeared in Mirrors & Thorns - An OWS Ink Dark Fairy Tale Anthology published by Catterfly Publishing (A Division of OWS Ink. LLC), and is reprinted here by permission of the publisher.

"Well, perhaps I'll send a card or two to some friends before we leave."

"Suit yourself, they're already stamped, buck each or five for four fifty. You can drop 'em off at the desk before three, and they'll go out with the afternoon mail."

"Thanks," Cecelia said in response to the gruff offer. "What I was wanting to do now is take a walk along the shore. Can you suggest the best way for me to go?"

"I can try to explain it to you, but the best thing is to buy a tour map which'll show you all the trails. You can take it with you so as not to get lost. Only a buck – to cover the cost, you see," explained Mrs. Merman.

Cecelia gave in to the inevitable and plopped a dollar down on the counter. The old lady opened the cash register drawer and pulled out a single sheet of green paper containing a line drawing of the cove. She laid it out on the counter. Cecelia studied the crude drawing for a minute.

"If you ask me," Mrs. Merman interjected, "I'd recommend the Serenity Trail, if you're lookin' to go down to the water's edge. Not too steep and the shore is purty smooth where it comes out. Now, if you want a good look out to sea, head along the Lookout Trail. It runs up along the cliff to its highest point."

She traced the routes out with a gnarled finger. "Got a bench to sit on and you'll be able to see the boats comin' in. Wouldn't try that Adventure Trail, though. Don't know why I even put it on the silly map. Awful steep and the coastline is very rocky where it comes out. Can't see much up that away 'cause of the cliff." She pushed the map toward Cecelia. "No, I wouldn't recommend it at all. Could be treacherous for a purty young thing like you. Better safe than sorry."

Cecelia repeated the words in her mind. *Better safe than sorry.* That summed up her approach to life and what was

24

weighing so heavily on her mind. She felt everything she had ever done was safe. She had never really tested the boundaries – always played it safe- stayed at home, got a teaching degree instead of studying marine biology, married a hometown boy with a good job at the local factory instead of taking a year to travel in Europe. None of that was necessarily wrong, but she sometimes felt she was letting life pass her by.

"Thanks," she said, picking up the map. "I think I'll just head out and see where I end up."

"One more thing, dearie," added the old woman, "the sun sets fast 'round here, real fast. The dark sneaks up on you an' you'll be in the shadows before you know it and that's when you don't want to be down along the water. The shadows can play mean tricks on you. No, best not be caught down there at dusk. Not telling you what to do or nothin', just a friendly warning so's to speak."

"Thanks, again," Cecelia said, "OK to leave my things here?"

"Whatever suits you. Just set 'em on the chair and I'll keep an eye on 'em."

Cecelia stuffed her purse in her shopping bag and placed it on the chair, then folded the map and stowed it in her pocket. She walked out onto the porch and surveyed her options. *Better safe than sorry?* The Adventure Trail lay straight ahead. Maybe things will change. *Perhaps this trip will signal a new beginning.* She picked her way down the steep path and soon reached the shore. Although the trail twisted through a steep crevice as it descended, it came out directly below the inn at the center of the cove's wide arc. Looking back up the bluff, she realized just how far above the water the inn was situated. The water surged upon the shore. The soft shrushing she had heard from the porch now swelled in her ears, almost drowning out the calls of the seagulls. The odor of fish, salt, and seaweed filled her head.

Just as Mrs. Merman had described, the shore to her right got progressively flatter as it ran out to the distant point. Pinniped Harbor lay just beyond. To her left, the shore receded into a jumble of sea-scoured rocks and boulders until it ended in a sheer cliff.

Cecelia contemplated her next move. *Right or left? Vanilla or rocky road?* She pulled the map from her pocket, studying it a moment. She turned to the left. A surge of cold Atlantic water rolled over her sneakers. She jumped back instinctively. Too late. Her feet were soaked. She stared at them as if they belonged to someone else, then giggled. *Mrs. Merman was right, these are indeed treacherous waters. Sometimes, you can't have an adventure without getting something wet.* Cecelia walked along the shoreline, picking her way among the rocks, occasionally holding out her arms for balance, like a tightrope walker. She had spied a column of rock jutting up from the rubble and decided to try to make it at least that. The uneven, slippery rocks required her to keep her eyes glued on her feet, limiting her opportunities to look ahead. She paused, peering into the clear pools of water at her feet. Examining the creatures within, she regretted not becoming a marine biologist.

She had just finished watching a small hermit crab disappear into a forest of waving sea weed when she looked up to see a man at the water's edge just ahead. He stood motionless, facing the ocean. Cecelia was so startled she almost lost her balance, one foot stepping backward into an ankle deep pool of water. Even though she let out a loud yelp, the man did not move. She looked for any sign that he was aware of her presence. *Surely he heard me. Where did he come from? Isn't he standing where the column of rock should be? Has he been there all the time and I mistook him for a rock?* She continued to look at him, but could detect no movement. All the time, she had worked her way along the shore, she had kept her eye on that rock as a reference point. She had seen it clearly in the sunlight when she started out. Now, the twilight crept out from the cliff base. *Maybe it was an optical illusion.* She remembered the old lady's words: 'The shadows can play mean tricks on you.'

Cecelia continued to move along, keeping one eye on the rocks at her feet and one on the man. *Should I turn back? Better safe than sorry, or was it safe and sorry?* She felt drawn toward the man, her feet seeming to move on their own. He still had not moved. She stopped as she reached a large flat stone. Able to relax, she took the time to take a good look. His deep, gentle brown eyes, which she could now clearly see, stared resolutely over the water. The plain, loose fitting clothes of a fisherman covered his frame but did not hide his muscular frame. His complexion spoke of a life spent outdoors, yet without a blemish or the ruddy hue of a fisherman. Thick, close-cropped black hair covered his head. He had fine features. As he turned his head to look at her, she detected an amiable smile on his lips. Cecelia found him altogether handsome. Finally, she managed the courage to speak.

"Good afternoon, I was just walking along the shore." *How stupid did that sound?*

"A fine afternoon it is," he said, as easy and comfortable as if they had known each other for a long time. "Few folk are brave enough to venture this rocky shore. Especially a young woman such as yourself. I don't think you make your home in these parts. Am I right?"

"I'm a guest at the inn," Cecelia responded, pointing up toward the bluffs.

"Yes, that would have been my guess."

"I'm Cecelia," she said, extending her hand. She realized too late that she was standing too far away to reach his hand.

"I'd love to shake your hand, but I've a mild aversion to getting my boots wet. You will forgive me."

Cecelia looked at the man and realized that he was standing just back from the water's edge. The rocks beneath his feet were dry as a bone. She hopped twice and joined him.

"Now, I'll gladly take that hand," he said smiling. "I'm Dylan."

"Glad to meet you, Dylan," Cecelia returned, extending her hand once again, "I'm here because I took the Adventure Trail." He accepted her hand with a firm but gentle grip and she was immediately put at ease. He had a subtle smell of spice and the sea about him.

"You do strike me as the adventurous type – the kind of woman who takes risks on a regular basis. You do have that look of danger about you."

"Well, not that often," she replied.

"A woman not afraid of getting wet, I would say," he said looking at her feet.

"And you a man afraid of getting something wet, perhaps," she giggled, pointing toward Dylan's boots.

"On the contrary, Cecelia, I would very much enjoy that," he said, his voice taking on a pensive air. A moment of silence passed between them. Finally, he said, "So you have set your course for adventure."

"Yes."

"Rather than the safe route?"

"You could say that. Perhaps it was only because the innkeeper was so insistent I take the easier trail. I don't know, but here I am." She was growing more comfortable with each exchange. "I didn't expect to meet anyone."

"Have I spoiled your afternoon?"

"Oh no, it's just…"

Obviously perturbed, Dylan spoke up. "Just that you weren't expecting to meet anyone. Neither was I. Your innkeeper friend has done a fair job of scaring folk away from here, what with her talk of treacherous shores and shadows at dusk. Has she made up any other tales to tell?"

Cecelia was thrown off track by Dylan's comment. He was still holding her hand and she pulled back, but he did not relinquish his grip. "First of all, she is not my friend. I'm just staying there for a couple of days with my husband, James." *Why did I mention James? ... Why shouldn't I?* She realized she had been flirting like a schoolgirl. Her cheeks grew hot. Embarrassed, she wondered if Dylan could see her blushing.

"Forgive me, Cecelia," he said, releasing her hand, "it's just that she and I have a long history, most of which is bitter."

"Well, I am sorry about all that, but it's hardly a concern for me. As I said, I'm only here a short while and regardless of what I think about Mrs. Merman or you, I don't think it's a good thing to get involved in other peoples' troubles. Nothing against you, but you can appreciate where I'm coming from, can't you?"

"Of course, I can respect that, Cecelia. It's just that I sensed you were an adventurer, someone who would take a risk to help someone in need. Someone such as me."

"Me, help you? I don't think so. Besides, that's not me. This has been more excitement than I've had in five years."

"But you long for it, don't you?

"Just an idle fancy. I'm really a coward at heart. I may dream about such things, but taking the Adventure Trail down to the beach is about my limit"

The shadows grew longer, creeping over rocks and into the water. He gazed intently at her, reaching out his hand.

"Please, hear me out. I would not ask if I could do this on my own, but as it is, I am forever cursed unless I can find someone to help me. Few come this way and I can't let any opportunity slip past. Just hear me out."

This man is dangerous. I should leave. She could feel her resistance fading. The more she looked at him, the more beautiful he seemed and the more she was drawn to him. She stepped forward, heart racing. Dylan lifted his hand and caressed her face. His touch dazzled her senses.

In an instant, she was no longer standing on the rocky beach. Naked, she glided through the water, Dylan at her side. Her body tingled with excitement. They swam through the water effortlessly, bodies undulating through the waves until they came to an island. They pulled themselves from the water and lay on the soft sand. The sun warmed her body. She rolled to her side to embrace Dylan.

"Forgive me." The sound of Dylan's voice startled her. She was once again standing in the shadows on the rocky shore of the cove. Her knees buckled and Dylan quickly grasped her, preventing a fall to the rocks. Cecelia's head reeled. *What just happened?*

"A Selkie trick. A glimpse of what could be. Unfair perhaps, but necessary in my situation. How else could I convince you to listen to me?" Cecelia tried to pull away from Dylan, but he held her close. "Leave me now if you choose, I will not prevent it. No more Selkie intrigue. I promise."

"Selkie? Like in Selkie Cove? Is it named after your family" Cecelia asked. *What am I doing? This is ridiculous. No good can possibly come from this. Better safe than sorry. Better safe than sorry? If I go back now it will be safe from here on. If I stay...*

"In a manner. Shall I explain?" he asked.

Cecelia nodded, not sure what to expect.

"What I will tell you may sound like the sad ramblings of a madman. I assure I'm not mad and what you are about to hear is real and true. You must be willing to suspend your reliance on every safe thing you have been told, and accept that there are things that exist in this world that defy your common beliefs."

"Is this going to get weird?" *It already has!*

"We Selkie are an ancient race of shape shifters. Our usual appearance is that of a seal, but we sometimes come to land and shed our sealskin to take human form. We are free to roam about freely for up to seven days before we must return to the sea. There is, however, one thing we fear. A sealskin, lost or stolen, dooms a Selkie to remain in human form until it can be recovered. After seven days, a Selkie can touch neither sea nor earth unless it marries a human and accepts the shelter of a human abode. Otherwise, the only place it can remain is on solid rock. Thus stranded, in the light of day or in the dark of night, a selkie must take the form of stone. Only at dawn and dusk, when the world is between day and night, can the Selkie retake its human form, but it must remain on rock. Why risk such a fate? The sensations we experience in human form are quite pleasurable. For that reason, even though we realize the danger, the lure of a frolic in human form is often too much to resist. Usually, we seek out quiet places far from humankind and the troubling complications that often come with contact. Nonetheless, the occasional interaction with a human is inevitable."

"So you want me to believe you are a seal in fisherman's clothing? I think I better go." She pulled back, but he kept her in his grasp.

"Wait, please hear me out. By human standards, Selkie are quite attractive. Selkie females are comely, both in appearance and manner. It is said that a man having seen one cannot bear to let her go. Believing a Selkie female to be a good wife, men will sometimes hide or destroy her sealskin, leaving her no option but to marry them. And though Selkie females make good wives, there is always a sadness in their eyes and a chill in their heart, for they forever long to return to the sea.

"Selkie males are rogues, known for their ability to beguile unsuspecting and unsatisfied women. They will sometimes venture out to find unsatisfied women for a tryst, lasting perhaps a night, perhaps longer, but always to return to the sea afterward. And that, I am embarrassed to admit, describes me."

"So you climb out of the sea and ravish beautiful women. That's some pickup line. I'm sure a lot of women fall for that, but not me." Cecelia pulled back, but could not look away from his eyes.

"Sixty years ago, I climbed the bluff to the house above. There, I met a young woman. Callously, I used my powers to beguile her and she gave herself to me. As she slept, I stole away to rest on the shore before returning to the sea. When dawn came, I awoke to find my skin was missing. Frantically, I searched, but could not find it. I looked up toward the bluff and could see her looking down on me. I realized she must have taken my skin. I rushed up the hill, demanding she return it. She said she would never give it up. She wanted me for her husband. I refused. She then said if she could not have me, then neither could land or sea. For six days, she stood fast, while I searched and searched. Just before dawn on the seventh day, I returned to this spot and awaited the sun.

Something in his eyes made Cecelia want to believe his wild story. "Why not marry her then? Surely it would have been better than this?"

"We don't make good husbands," replied Dylan. "I told her as much, not that it made any difference. For many years, she would come to me at dusk, demanding I marry her. Always, I refused. Then one day, she came to say she had married. I thought she might release me. That was not the case. She said from that time forward, she would never set foot on the cove. She said she would keep my skin so I would long for it as she had longed for me. From that day, I have only seen her at the top of the bluff, never on these rocks. I know she still lives in the house above, and I know she still has my skin.

"This all must sound too fantastic to be true, but you have to believe me. You must help me. Find my skin and return it to me. Please. I know what I did was wrong, but have I not paid a full price for my indiscretions?"

"I don't know," Cecelia stammered. "This is so... so... I don't know. I can't. I mean I don't know." *Damn.*

Dylan touched her cheek. She calmed down. "Time is short, dusk is upon us and my time is limited. You must go now, keep your mind open and you will know what I have told you is true. You must believe. Now go." He drew back his hand. Cecelia looked into his eyes. She could see the desperation in them.

"I'll try." *What am I saying? I ought to get the hell out of here and never look back.*

"That is all I can ask. Now go. Hurry."

Cecelia hesitated for a moment, searching for something to say, something to give voice to the conflicting emotions that roiled in her soul. Unable to say anything, she left, picking her way among the tangled rocks in the waning light. She looked back and saw only the column of rock. She made it back up the bluff just as full darkness engulfed Selkie Cove.

After supper, Cecelia moved into the parlor to relax on the faded chesterfield. Mrs. Merman had a fire burning. On the hearth, a large carved seal lounged, the black paint on its nose rubbed away from the loving pats of the guests over the years. It was not a particularly cool evening, but after the happenings of the day, Cecelia found the fire comforting. Mrs. Merman made a busy noise clearing dishes from the dining room. That soon gave way to the faint clattering of wash work in the kitchen, punctuated by the shrill whistle of a teapot. Eventually, all went quiet and the old woman, carrying a small tray with a teapot and cups, came into the parlor.

Cecelia tried to imagine her as a young woman in the passionate embrace of the handsome man from the cove. She was uncomfortable with the image, like the first time she connected the dots and tried to picture her mother and father making love. It was also difficult to imagine the old woman harboring such rancor toward him through the years. *Is his story true, or a fantastic ruse to beguile another unsuspecting woman?*

"Tea, dearie?" the old woman asked.

"Uh…" Cecelia stammered, thoughts interrupted midstream, "thanks, but no. It might keep me up. This is a wonderful mantle,"

"Yes, it is. My father laid these stones," Mrs. Merman explained. "Packed them up by hand from the base of the cliff. Used the same path you took today. He built this house, too. I've lived here all my life. I was still a child when he died. My mother had to take in boarders to pay the bills. When she passed, I took over and turned it into an inn."

"It's beautiful," Cecelia said.

"What's that, dearie?" the old woman asked, looking up from her cup of tea.

"The seal," Cecelia said, pointing toward the fireplace.

"You mean Dylan. Yes, yes, he is indeed a handsome specimen isn't he?"

Dylan? "Your seal is named Dylan?" she blurted in astonishment.

"That's what I said. Did you get some sand in your ears during your little adventure today?"

"No, I just didn't expect a seal to be named Dylan."

34

"He was a wedding present. My fiancé was a woodcarver. Before we married, he said he wanted to carve something special for me for our wedding day. He asked what I wanted and I told him my heart's desire was a seal. I told him it was just what I needed to dress up the parlor. He carved the beautiful creature you see here, for me. So from that point on, I had a husband and Dylan. He has been with me ever since, the seal, that is. My husband, God rest his soul, died some years ago."

"His head is turned to the cove. D'you think he longs to return to the sea?" asked Cecelia.

"He is where he is supposed to be," the old woman said sternly, leaning forward in her chair. "Sitting right there on those stones. He has all his needs and wants right there."

Cecelia was surprised by the old woman's sharp reaction. The conversation came to an awkward halt and the two sat in silence. She stared into the flames with heavy eyes. The seal's head seemed to nod in the flickering light. Soon her own head was nodding.

"If you will excuse me, Mrs. Merman, I think I'll head upstairs and wait for James in my room."

"You go ahead dearie. There's a guest pantry just over there," she cooed, lifting a bony finger from her cup in the direction of the front desk. "There's drinks, ice and other goodies if you get hungry during the night, or day, for that matter. The prices are posted. We use the honor system, just write down what you got along with a room number and we'll settle up at checkout."

"Thanks, I doubt I'll need anything after tonight's fish chowder, but James may be hungry when he gets in. I'll let him know."

"Well, sleep tight, dearie."

Cecelia trudged up the stairs to her room. Images of the day's events swirled through her head as she prepared for bed. She plopped down on the mattress, fully intending to wait up for James. She fell asleep almost as soon as her head touched the pillow.

Bits and pieces of dreams danced through her mind as she slept. They coalesced into a clear image. She was standing on the rocky shelf at the base of the cliff below the inn. A late morning sun shone down. She felt the warmth of the rock wall behind her. A twenty foot swath of jumbled rocks stretched in front of her to the water. Almost at the water's edge, a large seal lay on its belly, facing the sea. She watched as it slowly raised its head, looking to the sky. Up and up the seal stretched, arching its back until she thought surely it would break. A pink line appeared at the base of the seal's neck and slowly ran up its head and down its straining back. The ebony sheath slipped easily to either side, revealing pink skin. It continued to peel away, revealing a man who stood erect in the sun, arms raised toward the sky. He stepped out of the membrane which encircled his feet. His athletic body glistened in the light. Dropping to one knee, he gathered the pelt, folded it into a compact bundle and laid it to the side. He prized up a flat rock, scooped out the sand and gravel to form a depression. In this, he placed his bundle, then placed the rock over it. As his body dried in the soft breeze, a rich tone replaced the baby pink of his newborn skin. Raven hair had sprouted and covered his head. He stood up and turned toward the cliff ...

Dylan. Cecelia bolted up from her sleep, heart pounding. Adrenalin tingled through her body. She put her arms down to steady herself in the soft mattress. One fell on James. She held her breath, trying not to tremble. She waited a moment to see if she had awakened him. He did not move. She watched him for a moment. He was the safe decision. *What am I to do?*

Convinced he was asleep, she eased out of bed, tapping her feet lightly around on the floor for her slippers. Finding them, she slipped her feet in, plucked her nightgown from the bedpost, and pulled it over her head. A sliver of dim light from the hall revealed where the door stood. She inched her way through the darkness, holding her arms out until her fingers made contact with it. She flipped the lock and crept out into the hall. She picked her way down the steps, placing her feet close to the sides, hoping to keep the creaks and groans to a minimum. Once at the bottom, she went directly into the parlor.

The fire was burning low, but still shed enough light to allow Cecelia to navigate the parlor. She knelt down in front of the carving, now an ink blot against the red glow of the dying embers. She stared at it for the longest time. *What am I doing? Has this all been a dream?* She reached out. Her fingers touched the surface, still warm from the heat of the fireplace. She ran her hand along its softly curving form, feeling its smoothness. Grasping the seal with both hands, she hefted it from the hearth and set it on the floor next to her. Its weight almost pulled her over. She leaned forward and examined the hearth. All the fireplace stones were joined tight with mortar except for the one on which the carving had rested. Here, she found a fine line of separation. Where it met the upright stones of the surround, there was just enough space to allow her to wrap her slender fingers around its edge. She tugged up on the stone, revealing a compartment beneath. Perhaps the old woman's father had devised it as a repository for valuables. She peeked inside. Cecelia's heart pounded. There lay a greyish bundle. *Can this really be?* She removed it, then carefully lowered the stone back into place. Rocking back on her heels, she held the silky sealskin tightly to her chest, stroking its fine fur with her hands. Tears welled in her eyes.

Cecelia took care to set the parlor back in good order, insuring that no trace of her activities would be noticed. She lay awake, unable to quell the thoughts and images that swirled in her head. When James got up, she pretended to be asleep and remained in bed until the morning sunlight began to fill the room. She dressed and went down to the dining room for the continental breakfast.

"Sleep well?" Mrs. Merman asked, placing a glass of orange juice on the table.

"Yes."

"Thought I heard someone moving around in the wee hours."

"Oh, uh, I did wake up and came down to see if I could find something to help me get back to sleep."

"Did you?"

"What?"

"Find what you were looking for?"

"I think so. Anyway, I made it back to bed." Cecelia took a sip of the orange juice to wet her drying throat. "I'd like to go back into the village. I saw something in a shop yesterday that I want to buy. Would you call the cab for me? I'll be back after lunch."

"Suit yourself, dearie."

Cecelia gave the cabbie directions to a small shop she had visited the day before. Finding it, she hurried inside to make her purchase. Then, she strolled around, biding time, stopping only long enough to eat lunch. About two, she called for a cab.

Cecelia did not see Mrs. Merman when she got back to the inn. Relieved, she went straight up to her room and made her preparations. The afternoon was slipping away when she came back down the stairs.

Mrs. Merman was behind the front desk. She eyed Cecelia. "Going on a trip, dearie?"

"What's that?"

"Your gunny sack there," the old woman declared, pointing to the backpack in Cecelia's hand. "Mighty fancy. All packed and ready to go."

"Well, you never know," she said, slipping her arms through the straps. "Haven't made up my mind yet."

"What ya' got inside?" the old woman pried.

"Oh, just something to slip on. Just in case."

"Just in case of what?"

"Well, just in case I decide it needs slippin' on I guess. Won't know 'till I get where I'm going."

"Where's that?"

"Down to the cove, for starters. After that, you never know."

"Getting' late in the day. Not much light left."

"It'll be enough."

"Best be careful. Like I told you yesterday, you're apt to run into things 'round here that can be mighty treacherous. Things ain't always what they seem. Folks has taken the wrong path before and paid for it dearly. Better safe than sorry, I say."

"I believe you, Mrs. Merman. Truly I do. But as you say, daylight is burning, so with your leave, I'll be on my way."

"Need a map?"

"Got one yesterday," Cecelia chirped. "Anyway, I think I know which way I'll be going."

"Suit yourself."

Cecelia bounded out the door and headed straight to the Adventure Trail. She quickly worked her way down, feet hopping from stone to stone. Once on the rocks at the bottom of the cove, she made a beeline for the column of rock. She paid little mind to the water, soaking both feet as she scrambled to her destination. Shadows still clung close to the cliff's edge when she arrived. *Good. Time left to get things ready.*

Cecelia slipped the backpack off her shoulders and set it on the rocks at her feet. She looked up to gauge the shadows as they crept out from the cliff toward the water. Soon they would fall on the column of rock. Unzipping the bag, she reached in and pulled out a blanket. Underneath was the sealskin. She had hidden it in her luggage last night after bringing it up from the parlor. Knowing she couldn't leave the inn with a suitcase, the backpack was the perfect solution. Soon, she had removed enough rocks from the shore's gravel and sand to spread out the blanket.

The shadows had reached the base of the column. It would not be long before Dylan appeared. Cecelia looked around the shore and up along the cliff. No one was in sight. It didn't matter, for she was now committed. She untied her shoes and kicked them off. Then she pulled off her tee-shirt and unfastened her jeans, allowing them to fall to her feet. Before she left the inn, she had removed her bra and panties. She retrieved the sealskin from the backpack replacing it with her clothes. Gathering it to her bare breasts, her whole body tingled. She dropped to one knee, arranging it on the blanket with the back slit open.

She stood up. Dylan had appeared.

"Cecelia, you have found it!" he exclaimed. He eyed her standing on the blanket. A smile appeared on his lips. "I knew you would make the right decision. As I said, you strike me as the adventurous type – a woman to take a risk. There is a look of danger about you. It suits you." His eyes searched the cove and the cliff above.

"I've already looked, there is no one around to interrupt," she assured.

"A woman not afraid of getting wet," he said, gazing at her naked body.

"A woman not afraid. I've made my decision."

Dylan cast off his coat and quickly unbuttoned his shirt. He began to tug at his boots when he saw Cecelia step into the slit of the sealskin.

"No! No!" he screamed, reaching out in desperation.

"Too late," Cecelia cried, the sealskin moving up her legs as she knelt down. "I think the Selkie life will suit me well."

Dylan watched as the sealskin glided over her shoulders, finally covering her head. The Selkie let out a soft moan. Helpless, he watched as she moved to the water's edge ... then disappeared.

THE GHOST EYE[5]

Standing in the service line at the local Post Office annoyed George. It had a peculiar odor which hung in his nose. To many layers of government contract floor wax mixed with the cheap perfumes and aftershave lotions of the patrons. He didn't mind waiting in lines, it was waiting in the line at the Post Office that bothered him. He could anticipate a rewarding experience for waiting in line at a favorite restaurant or to see a movie. At the Post Office, he just expected to wait to pick up a package that had postage due. George could not remember ordering anything through the mail or on the net. His wife denied ordering anything, but he didn't put it past her to have ordered something from one of her catalogues and forgotten. He didn't like lines and he didn't like strangers.

After languishing about fifteen minutes, he spied the Postal Service worker looking up from her station with vacant eyes.

"Next."

George stepped forward from the 'Wait here until called' line marked on the tile floor with duct tape. He handed the green postage due notice to the clerk who pretended to read it carefully as if she had never seen a notice before, pursed her lips, took a deep breath and trudged off around the corner to retrieve the item.

She was gone long enough for George to read all the latest information on Zip Codes and the new forever stamp. He was just starting to take in the overnight deliveries when the clerk reappeared. She laid a small brown package tied with twine on the

---

[5] The Ghost Eye appeared in *Frightening A Collective Work* Published by Sez Publishing. 2016.

counter, consulted her computer, and re-read the postage due notice. She then keyed something on her postage meter and waited as the information printed out. Leaning forward, she examined the curled paper.

"Five cents."

George fished in his pocket praying that he had a nickel. Obviously, he had already disrupted the clerk's comfortable routine and didn't want to create additional turmoil by asking her to make change. Perturbed, he found only a dime and three pennies. He sheepishly placed the dime quietly and quickly on the counter.

The clerk whisked up the money and made the necessary entries on the notice and in the computer. Without looking up, she retrieved a nickel from the cash drawer, laid it on the package and pushed it forward to George .

"Next."

George started to feel the resentment build as he pulled the package across the counter. It was always like this he thought: an indolent clerk, in some miserable little position acting insulted if simply asked to do her job. After all, he thought, wasn't he the customer? Didn't he have the right to expect to be treated as such and not like a panhandler looking for a handout? George wondered why more Postal Office patrons didn't go Postal.

He could feel the muscles in his neck tighten up as he mulled the clerk's actions over in his mind. He turned his attention to the package. Who could be so thoughtless as to send a package without the proper postage on it anyway? If it was some promotional gimmick or something his wife had ordered, there would be hell to pay.

He tucked the parcel under his arm and, holding the nickel between his thumb and forefinger, checked the date. 1941 – maybe his luck was going to change. Lost in his thoughts, George walked half a block past his car before he realized it. Turning back, he tossed the package on the front seat and fired up the engine. After pulling out into the street, he glanced at the package. It had no return address. At the next stoplight, George pulled out his penknife and removed the wrapping.

Within he found a soiled leather pouch. Beneath its patina of dirt, he could see strange symbols and markings. It smelled like an old shoe. There was also a folded sheet of paper with 'Uncle George' written in large script letters. Behind him, a horn blared. Looking up to see a green light, George lurched the car forward through the intersection glaring at the SUV in the rear view mirror.

At the next light, he opened the letter.

Uncle George,

I thought this might be of interest to you. I came by it on a visit to the Cheyenne River Reservation. The man who sold it to me, Henry Grey Owl, called it a ghost eye and said it had been in his family for many generations. According to him, the ghost eye is used to see into the spirit world. Ghosts on the way to the land of the dead must pass through the spirit world. They are not necessarily threatening or evil, but they are always to be taken seriously. At death, the wanagi, or ghost spirit, leaves the body. After four days, it moves on to the land of the dead. However, some ghosts refuse to leave, searching to drive out the souls of the weak and take their bodies. Sometimes they appear as a white mist, other times merely dark and indistinct; but through the ghost eye, a ghost can be seen clearly. Henry Grey Owl said not to look directly at a ghost; rather, try to glimpse it at an angle so as not to call its attention to you. Looking directly into the eyes of the ghost will give it the power to take your body and cast out your soul. I must confess that I did not have you in mind when I bought the thing. I was going to keep it myself. However, after I had it a while, I thought of you and decided that it was time to write. I have a feeling it is just the thing for you. Anyway, I thought I would take a chance, so here you are. Well, I'm heading off on a long trip first thing in the morning and I want to drop this in the evening mail.

Say hi to Aunt Louise for me
Ralph

"Damn," George muttered under his breath. He had not heard from his nephew since his wife and brother-in-law had convinced him to loan Ralph $5000 to pay for his tuition at Vatterott College in Quincy, Illinois. Ralph was going to be a Computer Office Assistant. However, before his first semester ended, he decided to find himself instead and headed out West with the money. George had not seen Ralph or his $5000 since.

It was just the kind of foolish inconsideration that infuriated George. He should have known better than to give his lazy nephew that kind of money. His brother-in-law, Karl, was always asking for money for something important like paying the mortgage or fixing the roof. Most of those times he needed it because he had used his own money to buy a TV or go on vacation. Sometimes he paid it back, sometimes not. Fiscal responsibility was not Karl's strong suit and it seemed that Ralph was so inclined; and here he was now sending some stupid bauble with postage due as if he didn't have $5000 of his uncle's hard-earned cash in his back pocket.

George picked up the pouch and slowly loosened the leather draw cord. He casually dumped its contents into his lap. It was some sort of crystal about 5 inches long, the kind you might find at any of the hundreds of rock shops that encircle national parks. Around one end was a handle of sorts. A leather strip passed through a small hole in the handle forming a loop large enough wear around the neck.

The crystal appeared to be very clear and symmetrical – probably cheap glass, he thought. The afternoon sun slanting through the windshield glinted off the object as if it were a mirror, striking George's eyes with the intensity of a photographic flash. He moved the crystal, but no matter what position he placed it in, as long as the sunlight struck it, blinding reflections struck his eyes. Finally, he stuck it back in the pouch, drew up the cinch, and tossed it to the floorboard.

He looked up to see the light turn green, but the driver in front of him didn't move. George waited while precious milliseconds rolled by. How he hated people who didn't pay attention to traffic signals. Didn't they understand that green means go? He should just floor it and drive the idiot right through the intersection. That would show him. He was just ready to lay on the horn when the driver moved forward.

**

Two days later, George remembered the pouch and retrieved it from the floor of the car. He brought it inside the house and tossed it on the kitchen table. Louise was chopping cabbage. George hated its skunky smell.

"What's that?" she asked.

George knew he would have to endure a thorough cross-examination regarding the pouch and its contents.

"Oh, nothing important, just something I had in the car." He replied, not really believing she would accept his non-explanation.

"Well, it doesn't look like nothing to me. What is it?"

"It's just something Ralph sent, no big deal."

"No big deal? We haven't heard a word from him in some time and now he sends you a present! I think that is significant."

"Well you may think it's significant, I think it's a pain in the ass."

47

"Was that what the postage due was on?"

"Yeah, I should have guessed some idiot would send me something I have no need for, or interest in, and not even had the good sense or common courtesy to put the right postage on it." George began to sputter. "Hell no, just mail it off and let me spend half of my afternoon standing around the Post Office with a bunch of strangers waiting on some brain dead clerk to hand over some useless bric-a-brac."

"Well, I'm sure he made an honest effort – maybe he didn't have access to a scale."

"He wouldn't have such problems if he hadn't run off to some godforsaken spot in the middle of nowhere. What is he doing on some damn Indian reservation? What does he expect to learn out there, how to build a casino and get rich? Maybe he could pay me my money back. Fat chance."

"I'm sure he is just doing what he feels he needs to do. He's working through a lot, getting in touch with himself," She offered in her most reassuring voice.

George glowered at her. "Well, he still owes me money; I would have rather that than this piece of junk."

He turned and walked out of the house into his workshop. He stayed there until it was past the time for Louise to go to bed. He had calmed himself to some degree, but still felt the residual anger. It would linger for some time.

He turned off the lights, locked the doors, and went to the living room to sit in a soft chair in the dark and silence of a house gone to bed. Moonbeams cut through the window, shining down into the room. The soft silver light cast everything in black and white, like an old movie.

George spied the leather pouch on the side table. Louise must have placed it there rather than leave it on the kitchen table where he had left it. He knew she had not looked inside. She would not have looked without his permission. The sight of it rekindled his anger.

Switching on the lamp next to the chair, he took the pouch from the table, loosened the draw cord. A musty scent wafted up as if the grimy sack had let out a breath held too long. He removed the crystal. Holding it by its handle, he examined it closely. The handle definitely wasn't wood or plastic. It felt like old dried up leather but he couldn't see any seams or stitches. George thought it looked like an old chicken's foot only a lot bigger. The crystal seemed perfectly symmetrical and without a flaw. Surely, he thought, this must be some bit of mass-produced glass that the Indians sold by the hundreds to ignorant tourists.

He ran a finger down the length of the crystal, surprised at its warmth. He had expected to be cool like most things that lay around air-conditioned houses. Perhaps it had caught the last rays of the sun and retained its warmth, with the pouch acting as an insulator. He touched the pouch and found it cool. Probing the inside with a forefinger, he found it cool also.

Raising it to his eye, he peered through the crystal toward the picture window and the moonlight. He was surprised to find the images were distorted like looking through antique glass. However, he could make out most things like the trees and shrubs in the yard and the cars parked along the street. The field of vision was narrow and it was necessary for him to move his head slightly to see things on either side. As he did, images would jump into view. They were much distorted on the periphery, however the slightest movement of his eye pulled them into focus. It reminded him of the house of mirrors at the carnival.

As he moved his head to the left, a figure jumped into view. Startled, George dropped his hand from this eye and peered toward the window. Indeed, there was a figure in the picture window. His heart pounded in his ears as he quickly recognized his own

49

reflection in the glass. Once his pulse returned to normal, he brought the crystal back up to his eye. He again looked at his reflection in the window.

He examined the image for a long while. It appeared higher in the window than he thought it should be and instead of being distorted like the other images, it seemed quite regular in shape. He pulled the crystal away and looked at the reflection. It seemed lower.

He studied it for some time in order to memorize its shape and placement, and then looked again through the crystal. To his surprise, the image in the window was much taller and seemed to be closer to him than the first time. He noticed a faint flutter of greenish light around the reflection's silhouette. He turned his head slightly and the figure disappeared. Peering aside of the crystal, George could again see his regular reflection in the window.

Looking once more through the crystal, the figure appeared to be standing about three feet away. Whips of green glow flailed about its silhouette. George could make out the details of its gaunt, sad face. Its eyes, which were grey like coals with a hint of smoldering red beneath their ashy surface, peered into his. He felt as if those eyes could see right into his soul. He pulled the crystal away and with that, the apparition disappeared.

George sat quietly for a few minutes, letting his heart settle. He looked down at the crystal. Surely, he thought, he was allowing his mind to play tricks. No piece of junk tourist-bait glass could really reveal evil spirits – no matter what Henry Grey Bird what's-his-name said! This Ghost Eye yarn was just hucksterism dreamed up by the Indians to hoodwink idiots like Ralph to part with their cash. Suddenly he was ashamed of himself. All this was just stress, fatigue, and moonlight. Ralph would get a big kick out of this, he thought. This is just the kind of nutso New Age crap the little jerk thrived on. Wouldn't he be delighted if he knew his uncle was sitting in this living room right now about to have a heart attack over seeing his own reflection in the window? Well it wasn't going to happen.

George stuffed the crystal back in the pouch, tossed it in the waste can, and went to bed.

***

He only thought about the incident a dozen times or so the next day. Each time he got just as upset as he had the night before. He hadn't been able to concentrate on work at all. It was hard enough being surrounded by idiot coworkers, without the thought of the stupid trinket Ralph has sent. He was glad to get home because his whole day at work had been a disaster. He had just snuck by Louise and plunked down in his easy chair in the living room when he noticed the leather pouch on the side table. For a moment, he couldn't believe his eyes.

"Louise, what the hell is this doing here?" he barked.

"What's that, dear?" came her response from the sewing room.

"That stupid thing Ralph sent!"

"Oh, I found it in the waste can this morning. I figure the cat must have been curious and accidentally knocked it off the table last night. Lucky, I peeked in the can before I dumped it."

"Oh yeah, real lucky." Why couldn't she just leave things alone, he thought?

"Well, I think it's bad luck to lose something someone gave you. Besides, gifts are special."

"Well hell, that explains everything. No wonder we keep everything anyone ever gave us."

George glared at the pouch all evening. He didn't dare do anything while Louise was awake. He resented her presence most nights, tolerating long boring descriptions of her days, but tonight he sat flipping through the TV channels, scowling as the images

51

on the screen rushed by, utterly unable to think of anything but his wife's annoying existence. But after she went to bed, he could be left to his own thoughts. He would be free of her incessant, mindless chattering. Then he would throw the damn thing in the compacter and be done with it.

Finally, the time came when Louise laid her paperback down and announced that she was going to bed. George flipped through the TV channels long enough to ensure that she had fallen asleep and then turned his attention to the pouch which had been patiently waiting for him. Reaching over he snatched it up from the side table. It felt heavy as if it were pulling away from his hand. He could feel the shape of the crystal through the pouch. The experiences from the previous night flooded his brain. The apparition had seemed so real, as if George could have reached out to it. What a stupid thing to get upset over. Ralph would be so smug to know that this stupid bauble had upset him so.

He started to throw it in the waste can, but hesitated. If he threw it away now, he would never know if his fear was justified or he had been duped. That would make Ralph the winner and he couldn't live with that. He had to look through it again to prove it was only a piece of cheap glass. Making his resolve, he decided to look one last time through the Ghost Eye.

The pouch lay open in his hand and he gingerly reached in till he felt the crystal's smooth warmth. Taking it out, he held the crystal to his eye and looked into the yard, which appeared just as it had the night before. Slowly, he turned his head ever so slightly to the left until he reached the point just where the image had appeared. He drew in a long breath and turned his head. There before him was his distorted reflection in the window. He felt the soothing letdown of relief and a sneer came to his lips as he waved his hand to his reflection and it simultaneously waved back to him. He nodded his head up and down and so did his reflection. He wagged his head from side to side to pop his reflection in and out of his field of vision. So much for Ralph and his silly bauble.

George stood up and his reflection stood up. Satisfied, he could now go to bed. He turned toward the side table and began to pull the Ghost Eye from his face when the image of the gaunt figure flooded into view, standing right before him.

"Not so fast," it whispered in a raspy voice.

George froze. Slowly, the figure brought its sallow, drawn face close to George's until its dull gray eyes filled his field of vision. George sensed the coolness of its skin and felt the clammy pressure of its hand as it closed around his on the handle of the crystal.

George's mind reeled and bile crept up the back of his throat.

"Who are you?" he managed to squeak.

"A ghost," it rasped. "I've waited a long time for this."

"I don't understand."

"Of course you don't. Fools like you have no idea. I will not stay a ghost, forever doomed to live without form. For too long, I have lived on the smell of food, not its substance, the sound of voices, not their meaning, felt the air I couldn't breathe. I have longed for substance, for feeling while you have wasted your existence. You don't deserve your life. You are a sniveling insect, crawling on the face of the earth, totally unworthy of body or soul. I, on the other hand, deserve life. I will feast on every morsel of life. You whine because you are inept and lazy, expecting everyone and everything to worship you at your feet simply because you exist.

"While you have wasted your life, I have labored in the shadow world between existence and nothingness. Always searching. So long, so empty. Watching, waiting. Now my time is come, I will not be denied. Remove your hand."

"I can't," George replied, "You've got it trapped."

"Remove it, I said!" roared the apparition, eyes glowing angry red.

"I can't"

"Now!"

George drew his hand back. It seemed to melt through the apparition's hand, which remained tightly clenched to the handle of the Ghost Eye. The ghost's peal of joyous laughter rang in his ears as he fell back. He watched the Ghost fade away, replaced by a flesh and blood creature. George recoiled in horror as he realized he was looking at his own countenance. The only difference George could detect was the look of exhilaration in the George-thing's eyes and a beaming grin on its mouth. George wanted to cry out, but found that he had no voice. Looking down, he saw himself, transparent and wispy as the evening fog.

The George-thing slipped the Ghost Eye into its pouch and turned to go to the bedroom, bumping its shin on the side table. It winced in pain, and then its eyes twinkled and look of sublime satisfaction a came to its face as it savored the pain and giggled childishly. George floated slowly after it to the bedroom and watched as the George-thing climbed into his bed, pulling Louise close, kissing her on the nape of her neck.

She turned and wrapped her arm around him and said softly, "Oh George, this isn't like you at all."

PHANTASMAL[6]

The foolish believe the phantasmal can trouble the living. Not true. We have no more substance than the vagaries of dreams and nightmares that linger on the mind upon waking. An uneasy feeling that evaporates like the steam of morning coffee. No, it is the machinations of the living that pose the threat. Not that we are not without desire to bend the future to our designs, we merely lack the impetus. While we may possess the psychic vigor, we miss the physical impulse. Consequently, we are quite unable to do much more than wander about yearning for the corporal comfort we have lost through the death of flesh. This is, of course, a misfortunate existence.

***

My dearest wife, and I were shot for three dollars and our mule. We were in our cabin above Deer Run Creek. I was in the main room of our cabin when the raiders, murderous thugs masquerading as soldiers, burst through the door, pistols drawn. A single gunshot ripped through my gut. Hearing the noise, Rufina rushed in from the kitchen only to catch a bullet straight though her chest. She was dead before she slumped to the floor. Lying next to her, I lingered all afternoon and into the night. Our murderers bore no anxiety of conscience caused by regret for doing wrong or causing pain. They left us to die without contrition or remorse, angered only by the pittance of their murderous gains. They were not alone in their anger.

***

There is a old house standing on the foundation of our cabin. It is the finer of the two that have been built there over these

---

[6] Phantasmal appeared on line in *Imaginova Magazine* July 1, 2016 and in *In Media Res Stories From the In Between* published by Writespace 2016.

many years. I can only wonder what Chad thought, when Melissa pushed the ladder out from under his feet. He had asked her to steady it while he climbed to the top rungs, two stories up, to clear ice sickles from the sagging gutter. He had instinctively grasped the rotting metal as the ladder pitched to the side. Did he realize in the instant before the rusted nails gave way what she had done?

I think he would have thought it impossible. After all, it was he who had pulled her body from the icy water. They had been ice skating on the creek when she had fallen through. We had seen Melissa's phantasmal roiling away in confusion having been purged from its corporeal home. All the while, he had knelt beside the lifeless body forcing his breath into its lungs.

There are those rare interregnums between life and death. Pauses, if you will, between the last breath, and the irrevocable corruption of the flesh. Divergences from the instantaneous, indeterminable periods, during which a phantasmal, having been purged from its corporeal limits can return. For most, the moment passes before they realize their opportunity. In that case, death wins out. Sometimes, however, a phantasmal returns and life is resumed. The living have a habit of calling that a miracle. That is what Chad called it when her chest heaved and she began to breathe again.

***

His body lies there, on the frozen ground. She kneels beside him, pressing her hands over his nose and mouth until he is still. I see his phantasmal welling up, shapeless, roiling in the confusion that always comes with the fracture of the temporal bond. There is no guarantee the body will be serviceable after such trauma, but try I must. As the last vestige of his phantasmal leaves, I enter. What exquisite pain! My throat shudders open and my lungs suck down a ragged breath. Warm, soft lips kiss my brow. It will take some time to heal, but I know I will make it with dear Rufina at my side.

As I said, no phantasmal can trouble the living. No, it is the machinations of the living that pose the threat.

THE GIRL IN THE HARVEST MOON[7]

Nestled in with the apples, squash and corn falling from the cornucopia; a round, pale yellow moon with fat cheeks and twinkling eyes smiled out at Van from the calendar hanging on the wall. He squinted to read the small lettering under the picture: 'The Harvest Moon'. Then looking at the date, he did a quick calculation in his head. *Has it really been sixty years? Sixty years since I found this place? Sixty years that I have stayed?* He smiled and shook his head.

He stepped out onto the weathered porch and down the creaking steps. Following a well worn path, he walked back to the shed behind his small cabin. Inside, he removed the old whirligig from a peg on the back wall and blew away the dust that had settled on it in the year that had passed since he last set it out. It was very plain in comparison to many of the whirligigs he had built over the years, but it was his first and his favorite. It had been painted and repainted so often, the crisp edges of the wood were well hidden. He spun the blades with his finger and watched as the two small figures moved back and forth in a slow waltz.

He carried the whirligig out into the yard where he had placed a tall cedar post. Removing a newer whirligig with a boy fishing from a skiff, he set the old whirligig in its place. He stood there patiently watching until a lazy breeze floated up from the creek to turn the blades and start the figures waltzing. He had done this every year since he had built his cabin; yet, he still waited in anticipation until a breeze set the whirligig in motion before he would turn away.

---

[7] "The Girl In The Harvest Moon" appeared in *Autumn's Harvest: An Autumn Fantasy Anthology* published by Fantasia Divinity Magazine 2018.

Back in the small cabin, Van pulled a wooden chest from under the cot. He pried the lid up, retrieving an old pair of boots which he set on the well worn floorboards. Next he pulled out a bundle of clothes. He unfolded and smoothed the tattered garments gently with his hands as he laid them out on the cot. Then, he took a soft brush and buffed the old boots to rekindle a shine on the creased and scuffed leather.

The low autumn sun shown through the window, casting long shadows inside the small cabin. *I've got just time to sit a spell and rest before getting ready.* He went back out on the porch and sat in the old rocking chair. His thoughts drifted back sixty years.

***

It was the first night of the full moon, the Harvest Moon. Folks from all around those parts had gathered on that clear bright autumn afternoon to celebrate the time when Summer faded into Fall. Before supper, the women set out large bowls of vegetables, baskets brimming with bread and plate after plate of pies and cakes. The men stirred huge kettles of burgoo simmering over open fires, sipped corn whiskey, told tall tales, and traded knives. The young children played tag, hide and seek, duck duck goose and sometimes tried to sneak up and stick a finger in a pie while no one was looking.

Just before dusk, after the tables had been laid and the burgoo had been stirred its final time, they all sat down for supper. Reverend Stanhope rang a bell brought from the school house. After everyone quieted, he removed his hat and said a prayer of thanks for the bounty that lay before them. The meal continued as the sun dipped down below the horizon. Pleasant sounds of talking and laughter, punctuated by the clinking of plates, glasses and tableware settled over the hungry celebrants, only occasionally interrupted by a loud thump on a table followed by a raucous hee-haw.

After supper, as the women and children cleared the tables and the men loosened their belts, the musicians retrieved their guitars and fiddles and tuned up. The highlight of the celebration for the young men and women was the dancing. Many who waltzed at the Harvest Celebration would end up planning a wedding after the Spring planting. Before the dancing could begin, the Queen of the Harvest was crowned. Once crowned, the young men could bid to be her dancing partner for the evening.

As everyone had expected, Moira Flynn, a beautiful girl with fiery red hair, had been chosen. He had worked all season doing odd jobs to save up some money and had bid it all to dance with the her that night. He had never had the courage to even so much as speak to her. But he had summoned up all his mettle to put up his bid. He imagined what it would be like to take her in his arms for the first dance, to turn and sway with the music, to feel the gentle warmth of her hand. His heart pounded in his chest as Reverend Stanhope opened all the bids viewing each and then viewing them again.

"Well, it looks like we have a tie," the Reverend called out to the crowd with a broad smile and a wink. "Seems here that Festus Brock and Van Ennis have put up the same amount."

While murmur ran through the crowd, his heart sunk. A tie meant a contest of some sort to see who would win.

"Arm wrassling!" someone had cried out.

"No, a foot race," another had shouted.

He watched, heart pounding, as the reverend raise his arms to quiet the crowd. How would the tie be resolved?

"Well," the Reverend said with a wry smile on his face, "why not let the two suitors decide how to settle this!" A cheer rang out from the crowd. Pulling a silver dollar from his pocket, Reverend Stanhope said, "Van, you call it." He flipped the coin high in the air.

"Heads!"

Catching the coin in his right hand Reverend Stanhope slapped it over on the back of his left. He paused and then drew his right hand away. "Tails! Festus, your choice."

"Well, I guess we'll pole the creek," Festus sneered with a sly smile on his face.

Folks had been poling the creek for many years. Rather than get their feet wet and muddy by wading they would 'hop' over the creek using a pole. All it took was a long sturdy pole, fast feet and good judgment. With pole in hand, one would take a running start toward the creek bank. Just when they reached the edge, they would plant the pole in the middle of the creek and ride it up and over to the other side.

Each had selected a pole to his liking. As he had won the toss, Festus got to go first, selecting a spot along the creek he thought he could clear. He grasped the pole in his hands, took a running start and just at the creek's edge lowered the pole so it pierced the creek at its center. Then, he jumped retaining his hold on the pole and swung up and over the creek landing softly on the other side. "Your turn Van," he shouted smugly.

He took one of the poles Festus had left on the bank, walking right up to the creek's edge. He looked down into the muddy swirl left in the wake. Pacing back ten steps from the edge, he took a running leap and launched himself over landing neatly on the same spot where Festus had landed.

Annoyed, Festus walked along the creek until he came to a wider spot. He looked down at the water in the fading sunlight and then moved back. Taking a deep breath, he turned to Van and said, "See ya on the other side." With that he dashed forward, planting the pole squarely in the center of the flowing water and glided in a smooth arc over the creek. On the far edge, he teetered for just a moment before gaining his balance. The crowd cheered and applauded while he took a deep bow. Then, he turned to Van and had said in a voice loud enough for all to hear "Well Ennis, its your turn or if you don't think you can make it, we can send one of the girls across to fetch you."

He felt the blood rush to his face. Without taking time to gather himself, he grabbed his pole and ran headlong toward the creek. When the pole hit the creek bottom it struck so hard the jolt stung his hands. It was all he could do to hang on. The water rushed below as he went up and over. He really thought he had made until his feet hit the bank with such force his ankles almost buckled. Pushing back on pole for balance, it gave away. For just a moment he wobbled on the bank waving his arms for balance, halfway between success and failure. Failure won our as he fell backwards into the cold muddy water.

As the water swirled around him, he could hear the howls of laughter. Everyone had rushed to the creek's edge to watch him crawl up the muddy bank. As if it hadn't been bad enough to fall in the creek and lose to Festus, he looked up to see Moira laughing along with the rest. After much sliding and wallowing in the mud, he managed to pull himself up on the bank. He stood there soaked in cold mud, hot tears of embarrassment welling in his eyes. With the crowd's taunting laughter ringing in his ears, he bolted through the onlookers, along the creek bank away from the celebration. He tripped over roots; branches whipped his already red face stinging almost as much as his embarrassment. He ran till he could no longer hear the laughter.

He slumped to the bank, sucking in air, his heart pounded. Still, the faint sound of music floated up from far down the creek. He stayed there not moving, his head hung low as his heart settled down and the sting of his failure faded away.

It was almost fully dark by then. He had come to a place where the creek had carved a small bowl between steep rocky slopes. A flat expanse of grass stretched away from the creek. At its edges, the outcrops of weathered stone rose up like great walls broken here and there by trees and sharp grassy slopes. Stars began to shine in the narrow strip of sky above.

The pale harvest moon was just rising. He watched it slowly rise looking as if it were coming right out of the rock. It was the color of fresh butter, and he thought he could almost reach up and touch it. It looked so large, filling the sky. The stars began to brighten as the sky lost its last glow of sunlight. For a brief moment, the moon appeared perched on top of the rocks like the reflecting ball on its pedestal in his grandmother's garden.

At that very moment, the girl appeared. It was just as if she had stepped right out of the moon onto the rock's flat top. She stood there for a moment then gracefully descended to the creek's edge a short distance from where he sat.

The moon had cleared the rock and its full light fell on her. She was dressed in white; her long hair flowed down to her waist reflecting the pale yellow light of the Harvest Moon. She stared at him for the longest time, not moving. Then she crossed the creek. She seemed to walk without walking, gliding like a skater on the winter ice.

As she approached, he saw every detail of her face. Her eyes were black as coal. Her long silky hair was the color of honey. Her skin was pale, glowing in the moonlight.

"Good evening young sir."

He stood there in muddy clothes, his tears coolly drying on his cheeks, unable to speak a single word. The only sounds were the soft burbling of the creek and the faint music from the harvest celebration drifting up the valley.

"Ah, the music," she said turning her head ever so slightly toward the celebration. Taking a deep breath, she closed her eyes, "and the scent of moss, buttonbush, wild grapes, and the pennyroyals; how I love it so."

He watched as she moved around the small clearing stooping occasionally to smell a flower or touch a stone. She held out her hand to a clump of cattails along the bank and a damselfly landed on her finger tips. Drawing her hand close to her face it seemed as if she were whispering a secret to her small companion. Then she turned to him.

"Are you on your way to the celebration?"

"No," he stammered, "are you?"

"Not really, I come here when the celebration is held to listen to the music: but, I have never been to the celebration."

"Well, I guess you ain't missing that much. Just a bunch of folks down there making a lot of noise over nothing."

"And the dancing? I imagine that is wonderful."

"If you like that sort of thing," he said shocked at the sharpness of his own voice. Then more softly, "I guess so."

"Do you know how to dance?"

"If I've a mind to, I can dance a right smart lick."

She came very close. He could see every star in the sky reflected in her eyes. The moonlight glistened on each strand of her hair. She wore a necklace of wildflowers that gave off a soft sweet scent. "Will you dance with me?"

Her question caught him completely off guard. For a moment, he felt a sinking feeling just as he had when he lost his footing on the creek bank. He just wanted to get away, but it was either run her over or head back toward the celebration.

"Well," the words hung so thick in his throat he thought he would choke. "I'm… I'm too wet and muddy. You don't want to get your dress all messed up and besides, I ain't going back down there." he stammered pointing toward the celebration.

65

"That's not what I asked." She said softly. "I asked if you will dance with me."

Her voice was so gentle, so mesmerizing, that before he could catch himself he blurted, "Well, if I was presentable, I might."

"Let me be the judge of that." She laughed gently and placed her hand on his arm. "I would think a young gentleman such as yourself would be very proud of such fine clothes as you have on."

"Now you're making fun of me!" He could still hear the stinging laughter of Moira in his ears.

"But young sir, I tell the truth. If you would only look, you would see for yourself." With that, she lifted his arm.

Looking down, he saw his hand protruding from a fine linen shirt sleeve. His gaze followed it up his arm where it met a soft black velvet vest. Then looking down he saw his coarse overalls had been transformed into a pair of fine woolen trousers tucked neatly into a pair of freshly buffed boots. Then she lightly brushed his cheek with the tips of her fingers. The cold, cloying weight of the mud lifted from his face.

"There, that should do." She said stepping back. "Now, will you dance with me, or have you some other reservation?"

"Well there is the matter of some music." He blurted out trying to gather his thoughts.

She put her finger to his lips. "Listen." The soft sounds of a waltz floated up the creek from the celebration below. She took his hand.

"It would please me very much if I may have this dance with you," he said, placing his right hand on her waist. Stepping forward awkwardly, first with his left foot then with his right, he took her in his arms. She smelled of wild flowers and her hair fell across his hand like a warm breeze. On the third beat, he slid his left foot over next to his right and stood with feet together holding her close. They retraced their steps turning gracefully as they moved with the music.

They danced while the moon rose high in the sky. After the sounds of the celebration ceased to float up the valley, they danced to the music of the night creatures. The bullfrogs droned out the beat while the crickets, cicadas and peepers provided the melody. To Van, it seemed but a moment, and even though they danced along the creek bank, the ground under his feet felt as smooth as the polished marble of the main ballroom in the grandest hotel.

The moon had almost reached the opposite bank when she lifted her hand from his shoulder. At this gesture, the symphony fell silent; the only sound left was the soft burbling of the creek.

"I must return now," she said, softly placing her hand on his cheek.

"But," he stammered. "I… I don't even know your name."

"I am called Ithil' quessir yavieba. But that's not important, what you need to know is that I will return when the Harvest Moon hangs full and yellow in the sky to dance with you as long as you will have it."

"But, I… I… " He wanted to tell her he loved her, but the words hung in his throat. The sting of Moira's laughter was still fresh in his memory. He wanted to let her know how he felt, but he was afraid he wasn't good enough for her to love. He looked into her eyes searching for the courage to tell her.

She gazed inquisitively at him while he stammered. Finally, placing her finger to his lips she said, "From this day forth, I shall dance with no other. But, the time is nigh and I must hurry. " She pressed herself close and kissed his cheek, smoothing his hair with her hand.

"Cormamin niuve tenna' ta elea lle au." She whispered , turning away. She made her way up the bank toward an outcropping of rock.

"Wait!" he called as he scrambled up the bank behind her, slipping on the rocks, the roots pulling his feet out from under him. Finally, he fell to his knees and watched as she stood atop the rock gazing at the moon as is slowly descended. She turned back to him, drew her hand to her lips then gave a soft blow. He felt a warm, calming breeze touch his cheek. Then, she turned back, silhouetted against the moon which had just settled on the rock. With a small jumping motion, she leapt up and disappeared.

He knelt there until the moon slid down behind the rocks and trees just before a pink glow began to show along the opposite bank. As the morning light poured into the narrow valley, he laid his handkerchief on the spot where he would build his cabin.

***

"Cormamin lindua ele lle."

Van awoke to the lilting sound of her voice. He had never understood her sweet musical language, but it always comforted him and he always missed it when she left. *All these years.* Night had fallen and silvery moonlight streamed onto the porch. She stood there in front of him leaning over, her face close to his ear.

"Awake, young sir. The night is wasting and the moon has already started its journey over the valley. The bullfrogs are drumming and the crickets are singing. Will you dance with me?"

"Well," the words stuck in his throat. Even after 60 years, his heart raced at the first sight of her. "I'm ... I'm not dressed proper, I've still got my work clothes on. You don't want to dance with some old fool in dusty overalls, I must have fallen asleep. Let me get up and go get ready," he stammered.

68

"That's not what I asked," she said softly. "I asked if you will dance with me. Besides, the night is short and I care not to wait any longer."

Her voice was so gentle, so mesmerizing, that before he could catch himself he blurted, "Well, if I was presentable, I might."

"Let me be the judge of that." She said gently placing her hand on his arm. "I would think a young gentleman such as yourself would be very proud of his fine clothes."

Looking down, he saw his hand protruding from a fine linen shirt sleeve. His gaze followed it up his arm where it met a soft black velvet vest. Then looking down, he saw his coarse overalls had been transformed into a pair of fine woolen trousers tucked neatly into a pair of freshly buffed, supple leather boots. She lightly brushed his cheek with the tips of her fingers. His face tingled as if a brisk morning breeze had just passed. He retraced with his hand where she had touched his cheek and found the bristle of his beard and the deep wrinkles along his jaw had melted away.

"There, that should do." She said stepping back. "Now, will you dance with me, or have you some other silly excuse?"

"Well, I guess if you're up to it, I am too," he said rising quickly from the old rocker. His legs felt light and he hopped off the porch landing at the foot of the steps. With a sweeping bow, he reached out his hand as she stepped down from the porch. "The night is young and our band is playing. May I have this dance?"

"Why of course. After all, I have been waiting a whole year for you to ask."

He stepped close, as he had done that first time so many years ago, placing his right hand on her waist. Stepping forward, first with his left foot then with his right, they began. The scent of wild flowers enveloped him. Her hair fell across his hand like a warm breeze. Then he slid his left foot over next to his right and stood with feet together holding her close. They retraced their steps turning gracefully as they moved with the music. He held her tightly as if she might blow away in the night breeze.

They danced all the night while the moon traveled high in the sky and slowly dropped toward the horizon. The night creatures sang their sweet concert, grander than the finest symphony. The ground felt so smooth they seemed to glide over it like figure skaters on ice. All the weariness of his years melted away and he felt as young and alive as he had when he first danced with her.

The moon had almost reached the opposite bank when she lifted her hand from his shoulder. The night creatures fell silent; the only sound left was the soft swishing of the creek.

"It is time to return now." She said softly placing her hand on his cheek.

"Yes, I know." He said sadly, "But I wish you could stay."

"Would that we could linger, but, the time is nigh and we must hurry."

He stood still holding her hand. Tears welled up in his eyes. As much as he relished the time he shared with her each year, he dreaded the moment when she had to leave. Since their first dance, he had not again attempted to tell her what was in his heart. Fear had kept him from telling her all these years. He could not bring himself to risk the humiliation of failure and rejection. He could never forget that night at the creek bank so many years ago. The sting of Moira's laughter was as fresh and painful as if it had just happened. For that reason, through the years he had kept his feelings locked inside. *How foolish, how sad!* But now, he realized fear had suffocated him, leaving him with a frustration and emptiness that he could no longer bear. He had been willing to accept moments of happiness when he might have enjoyed a lifetime. He knew now he must let her know what had been in his heart so long.

"Those many years ago there was something I wanted to tell you; but couldn't. But before this night passes, I must tell you because I don't know how many more chances I will have." He felt as if all the weariness of his life was waiting to seep back into his body. "I know I'm an old man, far beyond his usefulness and years away from youthful romance." His throat felt thick and dry. "But I loved you the first time I saw you and I still love you now."

"Amin mela lle," She said smiling, "as I love you and have loved you all these years. "I have been waiting these many years for you to tell me." She pressed herself close and kissed him, smoothing his hair with her hand. "Lle merna aut?" she said. "Shall we go?"

"We?"

Grasping his hand tightly, she turned and started up the bank toward an outcropping of rock. "Asca! Khila amin." She said motioning toward the outcropping of rock high above the creek.

He did not understand, but it was clear she wanted him to go with her. His legs felt like lead. Never before had she given the slightest hint that he was to go with her up the bank. He had never even tried after that first night when he had fallen down on the steep slope. Since then, he always stayed at the creek's edge watching as she lithely sprang up the rocky slope. Now she was asking him to go and he stood there as if his feet had grown roots.

"Asca!" She said tugging his hand. "Hurry!"

His heart pounded in his chest. His face felt hot as if he had been splitting logs on a wintry day.

"Please come with me. This is your moment. It will not come again. We shall see many wonders and experience many delights. And we will dance again and again at the time of the Harvest Moon. Stay, and we never dance again."

"I don't understand, I... I've got to get my things. I need to..."

"There is no time. Don't let hesitation and fear hold you back. Trust that you will find all you have longed for; all you have been afraid to pursue. You have danced with me all these years. Surely you can go with me now. Don't look back, don't think about it, let me guide you."

She tugged gently on his hand as he stepped forward. Each step came faster than the last. The earth felt smooth beneath his feet. Even though they had reached the sharp incline of the bank, his feet felt sure and steady on the rocky slope. At the top, they bound lightly onto the flat rock where he had watched her jump so many times. He gazed at the moon, now so large it filled the sky. He could see every detail as if he could reach out and touch it.

"Mela en' coiamin, are you ready?"

He turned to look down at the cabin by the creek. There, slumped in the old rocking chair, was a grizzled old man. Then, he turned back, looking into her loving face and he understood.

"Yes, I am."

With a small jumping motion they leapt up and disappeared.

LAZY CROW AND RED FANG

Lazy Crow was so named because he was very lazy. He was so lazy that he would not go on the hunt. He was content to eat the scraps left over from the fires of other braves. Lazy Crow was so lazy that his spirit did not dream. One night, after Lazy Crow's spirit went to sleep, his body decided to go for a walk in the forest. It had been a great time since his body had walked the path of the hunter. His body breathed in the air of the forest. The sweet odor of the pines filled its lungs and the cool air soothed its face. After a while, because Lazy Crow neither hunted or fished, his body grew tired and sat on a rock to rest.

While sitting on the rock, a spirit came along. Knowing that it could not out run the spirit, Lazy Crow's body sat quietly as it approached. The spirit paused and sniffed the night air into its nostrils. Then it said, "I smell a man, but do not sense his spirit." Lazy Crow's body sat still and did not speak for it knew that spirits were unpredictable and to tempt one could be dangerous. As the spirit moved closer, it could see the specter of a large and fierce wolf.

The spirit stopped and asked, "Why do you travel the forest at night without your spirit, for it is unnatural for a body to walk about without its spirit to guide it?"

Lazy Crow's body replied, "The spirit to which this body belongs has grown too lazy. It cares not to hunt, fish, or even dream. This body is yet young and does not wish to huddle by the lodge fire or sleep in the shadows like an old dog. This body longs for the hunt, to ride into battle against its enemies, and take the journey of the dream quest." Rising up, it said, "If you have come for battle, this body will gladly face such a noble spirit."

73

"I am Red Fang, of the Running Wolf Clan," the spirit replied. "My teeth are stained red with the blood of my enemies. I was a mighty hunter and fierce warrior. I was the leader of my clan. Two days past, in the stone bluffs that rise above the forest, I fought a mighty bear that had attacked my clan. I counted many coup. I killed the bear, but not before he injured me gravely. Broken and bleeding, I could not keep up with the pack and as is our custom, I stayed behind. My body, frail and injured, lies just beyond these trees, soon to die. The spirit of Red Fang is still fierce and it too longs for the hunt, to battle its enemies, and travel the trail of the dream quest." The spirit bowed its head. "Fear not, this night is not for counting coup. "

"Then let us walk together while the moon makes its journey through the night sky," said Lazy Crow's body as it started to stride along the path towards the high crags that rose above the forest floor. The spirit fell into step along side. As the moon moved along its slow journey across the heavens, Red Fang's spirit spoke of its ancestors and the glories of the hunt, and vanquishing enemies. Lazy Crow's body listened in deepening sadness that it had no such spirit living in it. Just before dawn, the spirit said, "It is time to return to my body. It will soon die and I must return so I can my journey with it to the skeleton forest to join my ancestors."

Then the body of Lazy Crow said, "it is not good that such a brave and noble spirit should travel to the skeleton forest so soon." They had come to the edge of the forest where the stone bluffs rose up to meet the sky. There, they came upon Red Fang's body, laying in the soft grass, caked in blood quivering with each labored breath. "Nor, is this the way for a brave warrior to die," said Lazy Crow's body kneeling down and lifting the injured wolf's body. "Come, we will return to the lodge where the spirit of this body sleeps." They walked in silence until they came to Lazy

Crow's lodge. Going inside, they gently laid the wolf in the spot where the sleeping spirit lay.

At the first sign of the sun, Lazy Crow's spirit awoke into the wolf's body. At the same moment, Lazy Crow's body turned to face Red Fang's spirit beckoning it to leap inside and in that instant, the two were joined.

In time, the cunning and bravery, as well as the compassion shown for the crippled wolf, earned the admiration of the tribe and they came to call him Crow Wolf. After many heroic exploits, Crow Wolf became the chief of his tribe. His arrows flew true on the hunt and his spear always found its mark. His enemies recognized him by the red fangs he painted on his face and they grew to fear and respect his coup stick. Crow Wolf lived many years and sired many children. His legend grew so great that stories of his feats were told at the council fires long after his death.

A TAX OF BLOOD[8]

Leysa and Yuri watched Osip hunch over the table, his quill scuffing over the paper whispering a harsh tattoo as he methodically listed the taxes due. He had arrived in the morning, scratching at the door like a hungry animal. He had spent the day with Yuri walking about the farm, assessing the livestock, the crops, and anything else upon which a levy could be placed. He smelled of dung and sweat. Spittle flew from his mouth when he spoke. She hated the twisted gnome of a man.

"Go on, you bastard," Yuri growled, "why not include the stones in fields if you intend to take everything? You and your master are nothing more than beasts preying on the weak."

"Watch your words," Osip warned, looking up from the paper. He stared into Yuri's eyes, "He does not take well to vassals chiding his attendants. Know this, fool. The tribulations, real or imagined, of you and your wretched family are of no concern to me. My job is to list everything according to his instructions and place a fair value for which the assessment is made. Nothing more and certainly nothing less. He is rather emphatic on this matter. I dare say your tongue will not be so quick to wag when he comes to your door to collect what is due." He returned to his writing.

Yuri hung his head. "Forgive my insolence. But surely," he pleaded, "can't you show some discretion?"

Osip paused, lifting his head. He raised his left arm. Only a thumb and forefinger protruded from the mangled lump of flesh at its end. Sweeping back a long, tangled shock of greasy hair from the side of his face, he revealed a ruddy scar running from his temple to his shoulder. In the center, all that remained of his ear was a ragged hole. "Need I remind you of his reward for

[8] "A Tax of Blood" appeared on line in *Fiction On The Web* 12/4/2016

discretion?" Leysa winced at his disfigurement. In comparison, her own scars seemed insignificant. "And your daughter, Ekaterina, how old is she?" he asked.

"She has nothing to do with this," Leysa said, trying not to let her voice betray her fear and loathing.

Osip let his hair fall back down. "Livestock, crops, females - all chattel. Makes no difference to him. Young or old," he hissed, looking directly at Leysa, "All to be assessed; all to be taxed."

"She is but twelve. Still a child. He will have to make do without her," Leysa pleaded.

"Perhaps, still, he will want to examine the goods."

"She is not 'goods'," Yuri shouted, pounding the table with his fist. "She is my daughter!"

"Enough talk," Osip said laying the quill on the table. "Your prattle is of no interest to me." He corked the ink well and placed it and his quill in the pouch hanging from his shoulder. As he stood up, he produced a flat bundle which he tossed on the table. A sneer curled on his brittle lips. "Dremoh wishes one of you to wear this." He taunted Leysa, "Whether it is you or the child, I cannot say." Then, he limped to the door of the small dwelling, the bill of taxes in hand. He drew a hammer from the pouch and nailed the sheet to its rough surface. Looking toward the sun setting behind the trees, he said, "I will be off. It is not his pleasure to find me when he comes to collect. He will be here soon."

Yuri jumped up and ran to the doorway. He watched Osip hobble off. When he was sure the crooked man would not turn back, he slammed the door shut. Turning to Leysa, he asked, "What are we to do? This time, I will not let him have you or Rina!"

"Perhaps we will have enough money to pay the tax." Leysa offered, not believing her own words.

"Have we ever had enough money? That misshapen pig, Osip, always sees to it that we never have enough. Never enough money to satisfy the devil. He will not be sated until he has had his way. Tonight will be different. Tonight when Dremoh comes, he will taste my knife!" Yuri pulled a long blade from his belt, jabbing it forward in a stabbing motion.

"This one does not die at the hand of man. Yuri, your blade is useless against him."

Yuri fell silent, hanging his head. "I would gladly give my life if it would free us. I am ashamed. I am not a worthy husband. I cannot stop this anymore than prevent the sun from setting. It is you, dear wife, who has paid most deeply, and soon Rina will take up the debt. If not tonight, then surely the next time. Were I strong enough, cunning enough, I would have found a way to free us, but I am weak and afraid. Would that we should all die rather to remain under this yoke."

Leysa put her arms around Yuri. "Perhaps we will find a way to escape this burden."

"How?"

"We could leave," she said.

"Leave what little we have? And go where? Another valley, only to become slaves to another devil? It is hopeless," Yuri said shaking his head. "No, this is our fate. Ours and that of all those who came before us, and all those in this valley who live under his oppression. We were born to this misery and are bound to it for all our existence." He looked into her eyes. She was still as beautiful to him as the day he had first seen her; yet, there was ever the look of sadness about her. It had been years since he had seen a true smile on her face, and he could not escape the belief that he had failed to provide a proper life for her.

"Still, we must have hope," she said. "Who knows what may come. We may yet escape."

"It is hopeless. We shall never be free of him."

"Yuri, you must not give up. Freedom comes in many ways, and not always in the fashion we expect. You must remain strong; if not for yourself or me, then for Rina."

"Leysa, you are our strength," he said.

"You must promise. The time may come when you will have to be strong for all of us."

"Yes my love."

"Now, daylight wanes and I must prepare," Leysa said, hugging Yuri briefly before turning away.

She fought back her tears as she walked to the table and snatched up the bundle Osip had left. She moved quickly to their sleeping room, drawing the curtain behind her. Placing the bundle on the bed, she removed her coarse woolen dress. Her hand drifted down to the bundle. She loosed the binding, peeling back the wrapper. Leysa knew a neatly folded, white linen robe awaited within as it had all the times before. Still, she shuddered at the sight of it. Turning away in disgust, she walked over to a small table on the other side of the room. On it, sat a wooden basin. Earlier, she had filled it with the water she had brought down from the mountain.

Enough light still filtered in through the window for her to see her pale reflection on its surface. *I am indeed a pale reflection. We all are.* Her once raven hair was streaked with grey, her cheeks no longer full. The scars Leysa bore began to tingle like a spring sunburn. *He is close. I must get ready. I must give him no reason to look to Rina for his satisfaction.* She dipped her hands into the still water diffusing her reflection. She bathed as the Znakharka, Oxana, had instructed before slipping on the robe.

Next to the basin, sat the small vial Oxana had given her. Leysa picked it up. Its surface was covered in spidery runes. The night before, after Yuri and Rina had fallen asleep, she had slipped out of the tiny cottage and ventured up the mountain to seek out the shaman. There, under the full moon, she had met with the old woman to plead for help.

***

"What you ask is possible," Oxana had said in a solemn voice, "but such a thing does not come without consequences." She had chosen ingredients for the potion from an array of pots and pouches assembled in a semicircle on the ground where she sat, then placed them in a small skuttle. "Fetch some water from the spring while I light the fire," she had ordered, handing Leysa a hollowed gourd. "Pure water drawn under a full moon must be used." Upon Leysa's return, she had poured the water into the skuttle and set it on the flames. "He has no interest in our kind. We have nothing which can be taxed and nothing he desires. You might say, we do not suite his taste. Yet the suffering of those under his control is well known." While the potion brewed, the pungent aroma of herbs mixing with smoke from the fire engulfed them. Just before the moon set, Oxana had poured the potion into the vial and handed it to Leysa saying, "Fill the gourd before you leave and use the water to bathe before he comes. Now, on your way if you are to be home before the sun breaks," she said, touching the hand in which Leysa held the vial. "Mind you, drink this down just before he comes to you and no sooner. You will remain awake, but feel nothing until the potion runs its course."

***

Leysa pulled the curtain aside and stepped back into the main room. Yuri was sitting at the table, head in hands. He did not bother to look up as she sat down. Neither said a word, waiting in silent dread. The world outside turned dark as the sun dropped below the horizon. Soon, they could hear the faint sounds of galloping hooves and the terrible clatter of iron clad carriage wheels. The noise grew until the din was almost too much to bear, then it abruptly stopped, leaving only the labored panting of the horses to be heard. They waited in silence, listening to the scrape of boots on the threshold and then the rustle of the bill of taxes as a finger traced its entries. Suddenly, the door flew open, revealing a thin, black silhouette standing in the murky, swirling dusk. Leysa watched Dremoh, holding the paper in his bony fingers, glide through the doorway. A vaguely repugnant odor, reminding her of the fall slaughter, wafted through the room. He stopped at the table and threw it down before Yuri.

"Your bill is due," said Dremoh in a low, menacing voice. Yuri held out a bundle. The sound of coins clanked as he dropped it on the table. Dremoh hefted the bundle, holding it at arm's length. "This is not enough to settle the levy."

"Then send your dog, Osip, to fetch the rest," Yuri pleaded. "Take what livestock and grain as you may, sell it, eat it, do with it whatever it is you will, but please take nothing else this night."

"Indeed, Osip shall return on the morn and take whatsoever is his pleasure, but there is more due this night than a bag of silver and some cattle can satisfy," Dremoh hissed. "I see Leysa understands as she has put on the robe, but I will inspect the other first."

"No!" Yuri shouted, rising up.

"Sit down, fool," Dremoh barked. "Did not Osip remind you what happens to those who displease me? Would you have Leysa suffer the same fate as he?" He sneered as Yuri slumped back to the table, then ordered, "Now bring me the other!"

Leysa stood up. "Enough, I will bring her," she said, voice trembling. She made her way to the door and stepped into the evening darkness. She called for Rina, who emerged from a thicket beyond the road. Leysa put her arm around her daughter drawing her in close. She could feel the young girl shivering. "Come, Rina, and fear not, no harm shall come to you this night. Remember, I love you," she whispered, brushing away the tears that had welled up in her daughter's eyes. Leysa continued to hold her daughter close as they walked back to the cottage.

They stepped from the pale blue moonlight into the main room of the cottage. It was dimly lit by the pallid glow of tallow candles. They stopped just inside the door. Dremoh turned to face them. He drew in a deep breath as his eyes devoured Rina. He held out his hand motioning toward the young girl. "Come closer my morsel." She did not move. "I said come, now!" he demanded, voice rising in anger.

Leysa nudged her daughter forward, whispering, "Fear not, this is not your time. He will examine you, but you will not suit his tastes this night." Rina took a few hesitant steps forward until she stood halfway between Leysa and the black robed figure.

"This one favors her mother," Dremoh said licking his lips. "Fair skin and raven hair. Leysa, you need no mirror save this one's face to see your own reflection." He stepped in close to the trembling girl. He circled her slowly, sizing her up as he would a prize mare. Coming full circle, he was once again directly in front of her. She flinched as he dipped his sallow face down to within inches of hers. He inhaled intensely. "Nothing quite like the aroma of the female," he hissed. A frown broke across his face as he let the air drain from his lungs. He straightened up and backed away. "She has not had her first blood," he spat, glaring at Leysa. "But, of course you knew that."

"You would not have believed me, had I told you. And so now you know," Leysa said flatly. "And now to business if you are to collect what you have come for." She turned and walked to the sleeping room, whisking back the curtain as she disappeared inside. Swiftly moving to the table she grabbed the vial. Oxana's words drifted in her mind, *'You will remain awake, but feel nothing until the potion runs its course.'* Pulling the stopper from its throat, she drank down the bitter contents.

In the main room, Yuri stood up and put his arm around Rina. "Let us leave while he collects his tax," he muttered, ushering his daughter to the door. She started to say something, but Yuri quickly put his hand over her mouth, "Say nothing, see nothing," he said. They stepped out of Dremoh's icy stare into the warm night.

Satisfied the two were gone, Dremoh walked to the sleeping room. Drawing the curtain aside, his eyes found Leysa standing by the bed. The room was lit only by the moonlight filtering through the window. She did not turn to face him. He sidled up to her, breathing in her scent. His heart quickened and his hands trembled as he loosed the ties of her robe. It fell away allowing the moon's glow to wash over her pale flesh. She stood motionless as he wrapped his arms around her, nuzzling her neck.

As Oxana had promised, Leysa felt nothing - nothing of the pain, nothing of the humiliation she had felt the other times. She did not feel the coarse cloth of his filthy black robes against her back, nor the chafing of his clawing fingers on her arms as he held her fast. She did not feel the sharp sting of his fangs as they tore into her neck, reopening old wounds. She did not feel the shame of his abuse.

He moaned as he drank in her blood. For Leysa, the sound of it was faint and far away. Dremoh paused, allowing her blood to flow down his throat, then abruptly pulled his head away from her neck. He gasped, staggering back. Leysa turned. She watched while he clutched his throat, convulsing. "What have you done, witch?" he screamed, black blood spewing from his mouth. "I will kill all of you!" he shrieked, falling to his knees, eyes rolling back in his head. She said nothing. He struggled to say something else, then pitched face first to the floor.

Leysa stood still until she was satisfied that Dremoh was dead. She retrieved her woolen day dress and put it on. Its coarse texture prickled her skin, signaling her sense of touch was returning. *I have little time left.* She picked up the robe and draped it over Dremoh's corpse, then staggered to her bed.

Yuri burst through the curtain. "Rina and I were across the field. I heard screams," he panted. He stopped short at the sight of the body on the floor. Then, seeing Leysa on the bed, he rushed to her. "Leysa, what has happened?" he asked, falling to his knees.

"I have killed him," Leysa said.

"How?"

"I went to see a Znakharka. I poisoned him with a bane she gave me."

"I don't understand."

Leysa turned her head so Yuri could see the fresh wounds on her neck. "No, Leysa, no," he sobbed. "Where is the Znakharka? I will bring her to you."

"No, she cannot help. The bane which poisoned Dremoh, will also kill me. We are free."

"But why do you have to die, we could have done something else. You said so yourself."

"I said freedom comes in many ways. Dremoh poisoned me long ago. The curse that ran in his blood, infected me and so too would Rina have been poisoned when he turned his vile appetites to her. I could not let that happen. His death frees you and Rina. Only my death can free me. Remember, you promised to be strong."

Yuri kissed her then, laid his head against her breast, enfolding her in his arms. She took a few shallow breaths, then lay still. He lingered for a moment, holding her, before raising his head. In the moonlight, he could see a smile on her lips.

FIRST FREEZE

There used to be a holiday called thanksgiving. Nobody celebrates it no more. Most kids don't know about it, unless the old folks talk about it when First Freeze comes. There was a bunch of other holidays in the used-to-be, but most of them have been abandoned or just forgot about.

The leaves have all fallen and the ground is hard. Frost covers everything in a grey velvet. It sparkles in the morning sunlight. Bessy's breath shoots out in white plums from her nostrils, evaporating into the crisp air. She ambles along the crumbling pavement pulling the rusty bed of a Ford F150 that Hank converted into a wagon.

My Gram used to sing a song about going over to her Gram's house. That surely had to be back in the used-to-be. Going across the river then through a forest, or something like that, was how it went. Sounded happy the way Gram sang it. Could'a been about the now-a-days cause there was snow and horses in it. But I do remember the song also talked about this thanksgiving. I asked Gram about it and she just said that was something they did back before the Changing.

I haven't seen anyone else on the road today. Not that I would. Folks don't venture out much unless they got to go to town. But today is First Freeze and later they would be going to join relatives and friends for the celebration.

My Gram was just a baby when the Changing happened. Least that's what she said. Seems that in the used-to-be, people could fly right off the earth and up to the stars. She said there was a place out there called mars and that was where they wanted to go. So the asternots flew off in rocket ships and went there. I guess it's still there, but I don't know where it is. She said they was gone over two First Freezes. The Changing started after they come back.

We're on the way to Mom and Daddy's. First Freeze hit early this year. Been getting earlier most years lately. Folks say the weather was hotter in the used-to-be. Of course, there's lots of tales about the used-to-be. It ain't that far to Mom and Daddy's. Walkin' distance, but I remembered Gram's song and the part about the horse knowing the way and all so, I asked to take the Bessy and the wagon. Hank was OK with it cause he didn't want me walking that far after First Freeze with the baby about to come. Hank put the big basket with the dinner fixins in the truck bed.

Our folks moved up to Minnesota from down south with the other survivors after the Changing. There was way more folks around back then and they lived all over the place. But after the asternots got back from that mars place, people started getting bad sick all over the place. At first the government thought it was rabies, but the medicine they give 'em didn't do no good. They say people was dying, then Changing in droves.

Gram told me in the used-to-be, people didn't change after they died, they just died. Their bodies didn't get back up and they didn't attack the living. That must have been wonderful.

So there was like a great big war between folks that had changed and the living. It's hard to kill someone that's changed. Not that you really kill 'em, cause they've already died. You just stop 'em by whatever means you can. It's harder than you think. Shooting 'em don't work, Burning them takes too long and they just go off setting fire to everything in sight. Cutting 'em up so they can't move around works pretty good but it takes a lot of work and it gets messy. Luring them into a pen or trapping them in a room or something like that works well if you don't mind having them around until they rot out or First Freeze comes.

We're just making the top of the hill and I can see Mom and Daddy's house. I grew up there. Mom and Daddy gave Bessy to me when Hank and I got married. Her ears have perked up now that the farm is in sight. Got to draw back on the reigns or she'll take off in a gallop. I suspect she sees her old friends in the paddock. Hank says it's a good farm. It will soon be ours.

Anyway, after the Changing war, there weren't many of the living left. Gram said that just about everything was gone, either because it had been destroyed, or there weren't enough of the living to keep things going. So folks had to go back to the land to survive. But that didn't stop the Changing.

After a while, folks figured out a hard freeze would stop them that had changed. Seems like they don't have no body heat to keep from freezing solid. Once froze, they didn't come back. So the survivors headed north where the First Freeze comes early and winter lasts a long, long time. Ain't hardly anyone lives down south anymore.

Bessy trots off to the paddock to visit old friends while we step up on the porch. I look inside the front window. No movement. Hank pulls down the plank nailed across the door and we go in. It's cold inside. We find Mom and Daddy lying on the floor in the parlor in front of the big window. Maybe they were trying to get out. Hank takes them out to the hill behind the house. We dug the graves a while back while the ground was still soft. Me, I light the fire to cook dinner. Later, we'll celebrate First Freeze.

SPIRIT PAINTER[9]

Untah started the painting ritual, as dusk rolled over the parched plain. Teheht and his wife, KaHe, sat silently at a respectful, detached distance. They had called for him; but, like all who sought out his help, they were timid and suspicious. They had waited until hope was almost gone before summoning him. Dust whorled all about, provoked by the hot breezes that swept through the dying grasslands. The bleak summer of drought had devastated the crops, and there would be little to sustain this family through the long winter to come. Sickness, driven by hunger, had spread through the land. It was only in these times that spirit painters were remembered. He knew if his painting failed, this family might not survive.

As the day's light drained away, Untah unpacked his belongings under the watch of their sad eyes. Shell bowls were set out, ready to receive the sacred ingredients. He opened worn, deerskin pouches to examine the powders he would use to mix the spirit paint. Each powder held its own significance. The yellow sun was represented by crushed sunflower petals. Ground lapis lazuli for the blue sky. Red for life-giving blood came from dogwood bark. The bright green of algae brought harmony and healing. White, from ground gypsum, insured peace and happiness. Regal purple extracted from hibiscus embodied mystery and magic. Finally, black, gleaned from the charred ashes of a thousand gathering fires, to paint the Telling Glyphs. In ritual precision, as he had done since becoming a spirit painter, Untah mixed and remixed each in turn for his sacred painting. Then, he set out the quills, brushes and bones he would use. He paused to chant a prayer over each.

---

[9] Spirit Painter appeared on line in *Flash Fiction Magazine*, 9/14/2016.

Untah laid the fire from the wood Teheht and KaHe had gathered. He unfolded a tattered blanket and withdrew a large bundle of moss. He spat on it, and placed it on the fire. Billowing smoke welled up, swirling with the prairie dust in the evening's breath. As Untah was engulfed, he inhaled the thick vapor, its pungent, earthy odor burning his nostrils. He raised his head and blew the smoke out toward the heavens, carrying his prayer upward. There, drifting forever among the stars, it would join with the smoke of the great gathering fire of the Spirits.

He knelt down, pouring thick, amber oil from a hollowed gourd onto his hands to prepare the delicate surface to receive his paint. Through the night, in the flickering light of the fire, he methodically created his complicated tableau, adorning the surface with symbols to entice the Spirits. Without looking away from the painting, he knew Teheht and KaHe studied his every move, striving to make sense of the symbols, hoping against hope he would prevail. They had remained silent, maintaining a reverent distance, but Untah could hear KaHe's labored breath holding back sobs.

A pale glow began to seep up from the black horizon. Untah worked in the dying glow of the fire to finish before the sun cleared its earthly shackles. He intoned a greeting to the Spirits as he poured the finely ground lapis lazuli into the shallow shell bowl before him. The dull azure powder transformed into a bright spiral in the oil as he carefully mixed the ingredients. Blue was the color of the sky. The spiral represented the never-ending cycle of life and a path to the Creator. Once mixed, he would dip his finger into the unguent, and then recreate the spiral in the center of the painting on which he had labored through the night.

Now, he reached the conclusion. The bright blue track spun outward in an ever widening arc. He chose a fine tipped bone and dipped it in the black paint. Starting at the very center of the spiral, he painted the Telling Glyphs along its ever expanding path. They revealed the story of all that had been. A large portion of the spiral remained unembellished, symbolizing what was yet to come. As the sun spilled over the horizon, he painted his last glyph, the eagle, to carry the Telling to the Spirits, so they might know what was and understand the story must not end now, that there was more to be told. He took the bone stylus and placed it in the dying embers of the fire. Later, he would retrieve its ashes for his leather pouch.

Untah chanted his prayer of thanks and prepared to keep vigil over his painting. While the sun slowly journeyed across the sky, he remained silent and still, eyes ever watchful for a sign. While he waited, he thought of Oolmawa, his wife, and Chenat, his son. They too kept their vigil, waiting for him to return from his journey. He missed them, longing to enjoy the comfort of his wife, and dance with his son around the fire. But it would be many days before he would rest his head in his own dwelling. After his work here was done, he would make his spirit walk to the four sacred mountains. Climbing to the high plateau that stretched out as far as the eye could see, he would add his Telling to the never ending spiral. Only then could he return to his family.

As evening descended, something in the painting caught his attention. He drew his face close to the symbols, searching for the sign. Beads of sweat welled up through the paint on the child's brow. She stirred and opened her eyes. Untah smiled. The Spirits had been pleased by his painting. He knew this child would live.

A MERIN'S TEAR

Bredon watched the embers of the evening fire glow brighter in the twilight. A rustle in the oak tree above signaled that Mavie had returned. His eyes searched the limbs until he spied the magpie on a low branch. He reached into his satchel, withdrawing a long tunic which he draped over a small bush. Mavie flitted to the ground. Cocking her head, she looked at Bredon first with her left eye, then with her right.

He towered over her. There was the hint of a smile on his usually somber face. From the ground in the thinning light, he looked youthful. She could not see the creases etched in his face from the years at the forge. The grey in the curly dark hair of his temples and beard was not so prominent. The glow from the fire glinted in his black eyes.

She flapped her wings, kicking up debris from the forest floor. Instantly, a misty swirl welled up, growing in size until it was almost as tall as Bredon. Its undulating iridescence mesmerized him. Abruptly, it melted away, revealing a diminutive young woman with cropped black hair. Mavie employed this cloaking spell when others were present, knowing the writhing contortion of her flesh during the shapeshift was most unsettling. She stood naked in the waning light. It gave an amber sheen to her dark complexion. Smiling coyly, she studied Bredon with her green eyes for any sign of a reaction.

"I would think the evening breeze a bit cool for you without your feathers," Bredon said, looking back at the embers. Mavie knit her brows, slipped the tunic over her head and joined him by the fire. "Would you like some cheese and a crust of bread, or have you already dined on some beetles?" he asked.

"What fills a bird's stomach does not fill this one," said Mavie. Bredon tore a piece of bread and handed it over. Then, he sliced a wedge of cheese and held it on the tip of his knife until she took it. She bit off a plug of cheese, then popped a bit of crust into her mouth. Bredon held out a small jug. Reluctantly, she took it and sniffed at its contents. Grimacing, she took a swig.

"I'm sick of perry," she said, wiping her mouth with the back of her hand. "I flew to the seashore today. If we follow this road, we'll reach Combrie by midday tomorrow. I'll be glad to visit an inn for some ale and a cooked supper."

"Most likely all we'll find will be pilchard soup. That might change your opinion of perry," Bredon said, stirring the fire. Sparks swirled into the air. "I hear Combrie is a busy port. We've but a few blades left. Hopefully, we'll sell the lot then we can return home. Anyway, I'll buy you a proper drink."

"I doubt fishermen will be quick to buy your blades. Nets and baskets would be more suited to their needs."

"True, but there'll also be ships arriving with cargoes headed inland for trade. And those require protection by men who need blades. I'll find the local blacksmith. Always a good source of information. He'll know those who'd be interested in blades."

"New or old?"

"Both, if we're lucky," said Bredon, wrapping the bread and cheese and placing them in his satchel.

They sat in silence, watching the glowing coals. Finally, after the stars began to show above the treetops, Mavie said, "I heard something today. It came from deep in the forest that lies to the north of Combrie. "

"And what would that be?" asked Bredon.

"A sad, disturbing song. A lament such as I have not heard before," said Mavie.

"And what did it say?

"The language was unknown to me. But I'm sure this song spoke of deep sorrow."

"Did you investigate?"

"No, there was not enough time. After reaching Combrie, I decided to fly further north. In the distance, I could see a large fell and the forest that surrounds it. I had flown over a good portion of the forest when I heard the sound. I wanted to press on, but daylight was running out and I wished to return before nightfall."

* * *

In the morning, Bredon and Mavie shared more bread, cheese and perry before loading up their pony and setting out for Combrie. The sun was well up in the sky when they emerged from the forest.

Bredon surveyed the road ahead. He could see an oxcart heading their way in the distance. "Best we get ready for Combrie," he said, slipping his eyepatch over his left eye. Turning to Mavie he asked, "Daughter or apprentice?"

She shrugged. "Why not wench?"

"I was hoping to sell some blades and ask some questions, not incur the scorn of the townsfolk or have to fend off sailors too long at sea. Besides, I wouldn't have you thought of in that way."

Mavie smiled. "Well, an apprentice would be expected to do all the heavy, mindless work, but a daughter not so much. Nor would I have to wear those chafing trousers. Daughter it is." She untied the shawl from around her waist and draped it over her head so that it fell down behind, covering her hair. She fastened it around her forehead with a length of braided leather. "There, that should do."

They walked along for some time, until they met the oxcart. Bredon pulled their pony to the side of the narrow road in deference to the old man driving the cart. "Good day friend," said Bredon.

The old man pulled back on the reins, bringing the cart to a stop. "Aye, and good day to you," he replied. The stench of onions and fish wafted over Bredon and Mavie.

"Come from the market at Combrie?" asked Bredon.

"Yes, sold a load onions to the wyrt monger and a sheep to the butcher. Then I went to the fish cellars and bought some pilchards to smoke for the winter. Now, I'm headed home. You be headed to Combrie?"

"Yes. I'm a bladesmith."

"Well if you're looking to sell swords and such, I'm afraid you'll be disappointed. There's not much of a call for them things in Combrie. Now if you was making fishhooks or adzes that might be a different thing. But, since they already got a blacksmith, I expect that wouldn't do you much good either."

"Oh, that's what I feared, Father," said Mavie, trying not to laugh.

"Now if you perchance was to come upon Lyswen Fordón or some of his hardmen, you might find them that would be looking for swords and the like. He owns most of the land around here. He don't live in Combrie, though. He lives in the forest below Rýne Fell. None of the common folk know just where for certain. It's a place to be avoided. They says he dabbles in sorcery. He don't go to Combrie too often. Has his hardmen collect his rents and such. They ain't much more than brigands, if you ask me. Ordinary folk like me just pays up and stays out of their way. Best not to make no fuss."

"Why then tell me this?" asked Bredon. "Surely you don't want me, of all people, doing business with Fordón fellow."

"Aye, that be so, but how do I know that the mutton I just sold won't make it to his table? Or that my rents won't be paying for some of his mischief? Although he probably thinks hisself too good for mutton. Anyway, it's not up to me to stop a man from making his living. We all have to do what we must to stay alive, whether we likes it or not. Besides, I wouldn't want you and your daughter to run afoul of his bullies without some warnin'. And now I must be off, got to get these fish racked before dark. Good day." He flicked the reins and the ox lurched the cart forward.

"Good day to you," Bredon called after him.

"Are we turning north?" asked Mavie.

"No, we go to Combrie to find you a proper drink and a hot supper."

They continued along the road that led to the seaport. The land sloped gently downward toward the sea. Flocks of sheep and herds of oxen and cattle grazed in the rolling meadows. Crop fields, bordered by stone fences, dotted the landscape, as did the occasional small stone farm house and its outer buildings.

It was past midday when they finally glimpsed the grey-green sliver of sea between the sky and the raw edges of the granite cliffs. They faced almost north. As far as the eye could see, the jagged nubs stretched out to either side, unbroken, save for a notch in the far distance that jutted inland. The road ran straight to its edge. "Combrie lies down there," said Mavie, pointing toward the center of the gap.

As they neared, they could see houses and buildings clinging precariously to the cliff walls of the far side of the notch. A road wound its way up among them before emerging at the top and moving away to the north.

On the nearside of the gap, they saw men standing on the rocks overlooking the sea. They were shouting "Hevva!, Hevva!"

"Is that what you heard yesterday?" asked Bredon. Not waiting for Mavie to answer, he continued, "Those are the huers, clifftop lookouts who help locate shoals of fish and alert the fishermen on the luggers.

"I heard them," said Mavie, "but that is not the sound I was telling you about. The sound I heard came from the north, from the forest below the Fell where the old man said Lyswen Fordón lives."

***

Sometime later, Bredon and Mavie found themselves descending the narrow, switchback road, into the heart of Combrie. Dwellings and other buildings perched on rock outcroppings or huddled in rough hewn niches. At the bottom, a thin semicircle of rocky shore wrapped around the cove, protected from the caprices of the open sea by a natural breakwater on the south side of the channel and a sea-wall with two piers on the north side. Cobblestone fish cellars lined the south shore, waiting for the skiffs to bring in the day's catch from the luggers. Some larger sailing vessels were docked at the pier. A steady stream of workers carried cargo to and from the warehouses at its base. On the landside, wagons and carts traversed Combrie's narrow streets in their daily commerce.

A few inquiries led them down a narrow alley between the fish cellars and warehouses to the flattest and widest stretch of shoreline in the center of the cove. The distinctive ring of the blacksmith's hammer could be heard above the harbor noise. They followed it until they found a low cobblestone building. The forge stood outside under a broad sloping roof.

Bredon approached, while Mavie stayed outside with the pony. He waited until the Blacksmith returned the iron billet he was working to the glowing coals before speaking. "Good day," he said.

"Aye," the blacksmith replied, eyeing Bredon. "Good day to you. You have need of the forge?"

"Actually, I would have a word with you," said Bredon

100

"If it's conversation you want, the Lugger Inn is up the way," said the blacksmith, pointing the way with his tongs. "There'll be plenty there who doesn't have work to finish willin' to talk all day for a tankard of ale." He pulled the red glowing billet from the coals and began to hammer.

"I am not in search of idle conversation. My name is Bredon and I am a bladesmith. My daughter and I have come to Combrie in hopes to sell some blades. But not before I have the blessing of the local blacksmith. I am not wont to sell my blades at another man's expense."

"What kind of blades?"

"Let me show you," said Bredon. He went outside to the pony and untied a long bundles. The blacksmith, laying his hammer aside, pointed to a table near the edge of the shed. Bredon laid the bundle on the table and opened it. Inside were several swords and long knives in leather sheaths. He selected a long knife and handed it to the blacksmith, who pulled it from its sheath, stepping into the sunlight to examine it.

"No fancy butter knife this," said the blacksmith." This is a fine working blade, as good as any I have seen. Are your swords as good?" He returned the knife to its sheath and handed it back to Bredon.

"You be the judge," said Bredon. "Pick one."

The blacksmith picked a sword and slid it out if its sheath. He eyed it along the shaft and hefted it. "Straight and true, and perfectly balanced." He held it close to his eyes. "No cracks or pits. Beautifully polished. Truly, this is a sword for a noble warrior." He returned it to its sheath and handed it back to Bredon. "If this be your work, a master bladesmith you be indeed. I'm called Hamor," he said, offering his hand.

"You praise me too highly,' said Bredon accepting.

"I think not. And as for selling your blades, unless you've a stash of nails or filleting knives hidden somewhere on your pony to sell, you'll be no worry to me."

"Thank you, Hamor."

"I doubt you'll find much need for your blades amongst the common folk of Combrie. There's them that comes in on the ships that may have use for a long knife, but a sword is too long for work at sea, if you understand my meanin'. Then there's them that works for Lyswen Fordón . They's not to be trifled with. He likes his men well armed so who knows? If any of them is here, they'll be up to the Lugger Inn."

"I promised my daughter a proper drink and meal, so a stop at the Lugger Inn is in order."

"Well their ale is passable and the fish is fresh," said Hamor. "You might find a bit of pork pottage if fish don't suit. Then there's always pilchard soup."

Bredon motioned for Mavie to come over. "Mavie, this is Hamor. He has been kind enough to point us in the direction of the Lugger Inn. You're in luck. He says they specialize in pilchard soup."

"Good day to you miss. I'm Hamor."

"Good day to you. A fine forge you have here," Mavie replied.

"Aye, my father worked this forge, as did his father before him. The tools and the fire are mine, the rest belongs to Lyswen Fordón," said Hamor, sweeping his hand in an arc. "And surely he thinks highly of it, accordin' to the rent he charges." He looked at Mavie. "So, young miss, I take it you're wantin' some pilchard soup?"

Mavie gave Bredon a sly glance, then smiled. "I've never had pilchard soup, but my father speaks highly of it."

"Ah, well perhaps you might try somethin' else. Pilchards is a might oily. The soup takes some gettin' used to." He shot an admonishing glance at Bredon. "The Lugger has other fare as might be more suitin' to your tastes, young miss." He turned to Bredon. "The Lugger is a fine spot for a bit of food and drink of ale, but it can prove a bit dodgy as evenin' wears on and the ale has flowed freely. If you're lookin' for lodgin' tonight, my wife and I've got a spot inside. You can put your pony in the pen with my donkey. You'll be safe here."

"Will you sup with us?" asked Bredon.

"Thanks for the invite, but I've work to do well into the evenin'. Will you be comin' back then?"

"Yes."

"Well, let's get you settled while there is still good light. Dark comes quickly in the cove."

***

The sun had disappeared behind the cliffs by the time Bredon and Mavie reached the Lugger Inn. It sat on a flat outcrop above the warehouse road, convenient to port visitors. The whitewashed walls glowed bronze in the waning light reflected from the clouds sprawled across the horizon. They entered the dim room. It bristled with activity. The smell of cooked meats and fish mixed with the smoke from the great hearth at the back. Bredon selected a table in the corner near the door. No sooner had they taken their seats and leaned his bundle against the wall, than a short, stout woman with rosy cheeks came up.

"Call me Hertha. What for ya'?" she asked.

"Small beer if you have it," said Bredon.

"Small beer!" protested Mavie, kicking Bredon's shin.

"And something to eat," finished Bredon. He turned to Mavie and said in a hushed voice. "We need to keep our wits about us."

"Got a fine pilchard soup," Hertha said.

"What else might you have?" asked Mavie.

"Got some giltheads and dabs if you are lookin' for fish. If that's not to your taste, there's spit roast goat. We also got some parsnips on the hearth."

Mavie looked at Bredon with a frown. "I guess it will be a dab and parsnips for me."

"And the same for me, my good woman," said Bredon.

"That'll be a shilling and six," said Hertha, staring at Bredon, "before I goes to get it." He counted out the money and handed it to her. She turned and headed toward the barrels and kegs at the back of the hall.

While they waited for their food, Bredon took the opportunity to survey their surroundings. Most of the tables in the long narrow hall were filled with men, but some women were present. The sounds of talking and laughter, punctuated by the clinking of plates, mugs and tableware filled the room, only occasionally interrupted by a loud thump on a table followed by a raucous guffaw. A number of long tables, situated near the ale kegs, were filled with men hunkered over their tankards.

"If there be anyone interested in blades," he said to Mavie, "they'll be there." He pointed to the tables. A moment later, Hertha returned, carrying a flagon and two tankards. A young girl followed behind her, carrying a tray of food.

"Would you be needin' a place to stay for the night by chance?" Hertha asked, setting the flagon down. "I've got a place upstairs if ya have a need, but I wouldn't wait 'cause it'll be taken soon."

"Thank you, my daughter and I have a place to rest the night," said Bredon.

Hertha eyed Mavie, then winked at Bredon. "Oh, your daughter. I see."

After Hertha left, Mavie poured the small beer. She took a long draught while shoving the other tankard in front of Bredon. "Fair, but I would have preferred some ale. I hope the fish is at least as good," she said, scooping up the dab and taking a large bite.

"Well?" asked Bredon.

"I've had worse." She took another bite, "But it surely beats cheese and stale bread." She picked up a parsnip and smelled it. Pulling a small knife from her waste cinch, she cut it in half and examined its inside. "No rot. I guess it's safe to eat." She stuffed the half in her mouth. "Tastes better than it looks." She followed that with another gulp from her tankard.

Bredon and Mavie continued eating amidst the bustle of the Lugger. What little light that had seeped in through the windows soon faded. After Hertha and the serving girl lit the oil lamps hanging from the ceiling, they came round to collect the empty plates.

"Before you go" said Bredon, "I'm a bladesmith and have some swords and long knives for sale. Do you think there's anyone here interested in a good blade?" He placed a shilling on the table. "For your trouble."

Hertha snatched it up and dropped it into the pocket of her apron. "No trouble at all."

"A shilling?" spouted Mavie, "I think a penny would've been enough. That money could have better been spent on some more small beer!"

Hertha went to the back and stopped at one of the long tables. Bredon saw her pointing in their direction. Soon, a man stood up and made his way to their table. His pockmarked face was covered with a stubble of beard, his eyes bleary from an afternoon swilling ale. "You the one what's selling swords and such?" he asked, leaning over the table.

"Yes," said Bredon.

"Well we don't allow no strangers to sell things in Combrie unless they's paid a levy."

"By who's authority?" Bredon asked.

"Who do ya think? Lyswen Fordón's authority. An' he owns everything around here. Now, have you paid your levy?"

"And who are you to be asking?" asked Mavie. She closed her hand around her knife.

"I collects the levies and rents for him, among other things." He eyed Mavie for a moment, then turned to Bredon. "If you don't have the money to pay the levy, then a turn with her will do."

"Here's the only turn you'll get!" Mavie barked, jumping on the table. She lashed out with her knife, opening a shallow cut across the man's cheek. He cried out in pain. He reached for his long knife, but before he could draw it, Bredon swooped him up in his powerful arms and threw him to the floor. He hit on his head with a dull thud. "Behind you!" shouted Mavie, as two more men rushed up to join the fight. Bredon spun around, striking one in the face. He crumpled to the floor, joining his companion. The other man grabbed Bredon's head in an attempt to wrestle him to the ground. Mavie jabbed her knife into the man's buttock. He yelped in pain, releasing his grip on Bredon, but not before raking off his eyepatch. The first man, having regained his feet, pulled his knife and edged toward Bredon.

"Enough! I would not have this man harmed. Though I dare say, you would not fare well in a fight with him. Can't you see he has the tattooed eye? He is a man not to be trifled with." The voice belonged to a man cloaked in black. He was one of the men from the back table. He kept his hood up, hiding his face in its shadows.

"But she cut me," growled the man with the knife.

106

"Silence! No doubt with good cause, Gaut. Now, sheathe your knife and wait for me outside." He looked at the other man, "Pick up Flengit and take him with you." He waited until they had left before saying, "I am Lyswen Fordón."

"I am Bredon and this is my daughter Mavie. She was insulted by your hardman. He is fortunate to still be breathing." He picked up his eyepatch and slipped it on.

"I feared as much," said Fordón. "Sometimes ale dulls good judgement as well as manners. My apologies to you both. Hertha says you are a bladesmith. That seems an odd pursuit for a mage, especially one with a tattooed eye."

"Let's say I prefer the certainty of iron to the vagaries of magic."

"And the patch?"

"Too much turmoil follows a mage. I prefer the simpler existence of a one-eyed bladesmith.

"So you have abandoned magic?" asked Fordón.

"No."

"Only the most skilled mage can boast the tattooed eye. Are your blades the equal?"

"I let my blades speak for themselves. You be the judge, I have some here," said Bredon, pointing to the bundle in the corner.

"I prefer not to do business in a common tavern," replied Fordón. "I am leaving Combrie this night. If you come to my mansion house, I would very much like to see your blades and perhaps we can do some business."

"We would welcome that opportunity. On the morrow?"

"You can go with us this night, if you wish," Fordón.

"Thank you, but we have made arrangements and so will stay the night in Combrie."

"Shall I have one of my men stay to guide you? I am not easily found."

Bredon smiled, "No need. You live in the forest beneath Rýne Fell, I believe." He lifted his eyepatch. "I'm sure a mage can find his way there."

* * *

The sun had yet to appear over the eastern cliffs the next morning, when Bredon and Mavie packed up their belongings, said goodbye to Hamor and his wife, and started climbing the north road out of Combrie. The morning breeze rolling off the sea and flowing up the sides of the cove seemed to be pushing them along. Reaching the top, they could see Rýne Fell in the distance, well inland from the rolling fields along the coast, its high and barren dome jutting up from the green of the forest at its base.

They continued along the north road that led away from Combrie and the sea. The land sloped gently upward toward Rýne Fell. It was near midday when the road reached the forest where a narrower, less traveled road veered east into the trees. The main road continued on, skirting the forest on the western side.

They took the forest road. Once inside the cover of the trees, Bredon stopped. He pulled the patch from his eye. "Well, daughter," he said, "I think it's time for you to don your feathers and find out where Fordón lives. There is a good chance that where you find him, you will also find the one who sings the sad lament. I'll continue along this road. Find me when you are done."

Mavie removed her head piece and tunic. She handed them to Bredon. "Do I need to fly away this moment or can it wait?" she asked. Bredon just shook his head. Mavie shrugged. "Well, it couldn't hurt to ask." With a sweep of her hand, a little eddy of air whipped around her, picking up leaves from the forest floor, engulfing her. It evaporated as quickly as it appeared. The leaves settled, revealing Mavie, now in her magpie form. She sprang up from the forest floor, landing on a nearby branch and cocked her head back and forth before flying off through the canopy of leaves.

Except for a few billowy clouds, the sky was clear above the tree tops. Mavie headed toward Rýne Fell. The forest rolled out beneath her until it met the great ring of scree that had accumulated at the base of the Fell. As she searched, she wondered if Bredon's words were true.

Mavie was well beyond the spot where two days earlier she had turned back. The land was rising up to meet the Fell. Near the boundary between the trees and the scree, lay a large clearing in the forest mantle. Within, a small lake shimmered at the foot of a runout of rocky debris. A mansion house sat on the rock at its edge. She descended until she was skimming the treetops, flying in a wide arc along the edge of the opening. The mansion house was large, walls made of polished stone. An ornate 'F' was carved in the keystone above the entrance. She could detect no activity around the building. A broad courtyard, laid with smooth stone, stretched out to meet the lake. In its center A large oak tree stood. Beyond it, steps led down into the water.

Within the lake, a small rocky outcrop rose above the water. A squat, gnarled hawthorn tree clung to its barren surface. Its branches, bent by the westward wind, seemed to be reaching for the distant sea. A woman sat beneath them. Mavie glided around the tiny island, studying the woman. Finally she landed on a branch just above her.

"Come to visit?" the woman said, holding up her hand. "Fear not little one, I will not harm you." Mavie cocked her head back and forth, taking in the woman's appearance. She was small and delicate with a pale complexion. Her large brown eyes conveyed a deep sadness. Straight brown hair, still wet, flowed over her bare skin, coming to rest on the rock. "How I envy you," she said, "free to fly away. No cage to hold you. No master to serve." She began to sing in a soft voice.

Mavie instantly recognized it. Feeling an urge she could not resist, Mavie dropped to the surface of the rock and flapped her wings, kicking up the misty swirl. It was quickly carried off by the wind, leaving her standing on the rock. "I'm Mavie," she said, "you have nothing to fear from me."

The woman drew in a deep breath. "I am called Ula."

"It was your song I heard the other day. It is such a sad song. I do not understand the words. I pray you must tell me what they say."

"It is the language of the Merin. We are seal faeries, called Selkie in the south and Roane in Ireland. Female Merin can shed their skins to take human form and walk on dry land."

"It seems we are allied by nature. Tell me more."

"Taking human form comes with grave risk. Men find seal faery females comely, both in appearance and manner. A man having encountered one cannot bear to let her go, believing a Merin to make the best wife. To keep her from returning to the sea, he will hide or destroy her sealskin. Without it, a single drop of saltwater will turn a Merin to stone. I knew the risk, but the lure of a frolic in human form was too much to resist, and now through my foolishness, I am a slave to a cruel master. That is why I carry sadness in my heart, forever longing to return to the sea."

"So Fordón captured you?" asked Mavie.

"A fisherman caught me and took me as his wife. He treated me well enough, though I longed to return to the sea. Somehow, Fordón found out and offered to buy me. When my husband refused, Fordón sent his men. They beat him savagely and would have killed him had I not agreed to go with them. So here I am."

"I have met this man," said Mavie. "I had a sense of foreboding from the moment I first saw him."

"Fordón is an evil man, dabbling in magic, using it for his dark purposes. He does not care what harm it does. All you see of him is thin illusion. Inside he is an old, twisted creature."

"And what of you?" asked Mavie.

"He keeps me as his concubine. He shuns his wife, Gytha, forcing her to serve as little more than his house servant."

"Have you tried to find your sealskin and escape this horrid place?"

"It was here for a while, but now it is gone forever. I feel it inside. My situation is hopeless."

"I know that feeling," said Mavie. "I was once a slave to a cruel master until I was freed by a good man. Though he claims no debt, I have remained by his side ever since. Ula, there is always hope." Mavie paused, then asked, "And what of your song?"

"My song is my sad story. All Merin have their song," Ula explained. "When we gather, we sing that all will know us and remember us. My song will never be heard."

"I would hear it. Sing it for me before I leave. My friend and I will return this evening. If there is a way to help you, we will find it."

***

Bredon had been walking for a considerable length of time since he had watched Mavie disappear into the leaves above his head. The gnarled oak trees grew to the edge of the road. Their limbs stretched overhead. The thick foliage blocked out most of the sunlight, forming a dim tunnel that snaked through the forest. Occasionally, a path or dusty lane broke off from the road disappearing into the dense growth. The air was still and heavy. The smell of rot and decay filled his nostrils.

Bredon had learned long ago not to worry about Mavie. She had proven a loyal companion, able to hold her own, whether through guile or by grit, against the most formidable adversaries.

Still, he had expected she would have brought him news well before he had walked this far.

Without warning, a naked woman jumped out from the trees ahead. She bore a striking resemblance to Hertha from the Lugger Inn. She did a seductive little dance which sent her pink rolls of flesh bouncing up and down.

"My dreams have been answered," laughed Bredon. "Thanks be that I was saved from the sight of that scrawny Mavie."

A swirl of mist swallowed the woman. When it evaporated, Mavie stood in her place. "I thought as much," huffed Mavie. She hung her head, feigning dejection. Bredon retrieved her tunic and held it out. She reached for it, but he drew it back. His eyes lingered on her.

"Well, maybe I spoke too soon," he said smiling. He placed the tunic in her outstretched hand.

After pulling the tunic over her head, Mavie said, "We take this road." She turned, pointing to the spot where she had emerged from the side road. It was now a wall of trees. She furrowed her brow. "I swear there was a road there."

"Indeed there is," said Bredon. "It's an illusion. From this side, there appear to be trees. However, you came from the other side, where obviously it looks normal. Look closely. You can see a slight blurring. I sensed the same lack of clarity last night in the tavern when I tried to see Fordón's face. The old man we met on the road to Combrie was right. It seems Fordón dabbles in magic, though I doubt he is a real mage. Spells can be bought for a price, though usually not good ones. Fordón has placed a hiding spell at the entrance to this road. In this dim light, as poor as it may be, it is sufficient to fool most passersby, though I fear there are few who would travel this road. Tell me, did you find out where Fordón lives or will I fail as a mage?"

Mavie's face grew solemn. "Bredon, this Fordón is a cruel man, there is much you need to know. Come! I will tell you while we walk," she said, stepping through the illusion.

***

It was dusk when Bredon and Mavie reached Fordón's mansion house. Mavie was surprised to see that Ula was still on the island. They left the pony at the edge of the courtyard and approached the entrance. Bredon grabbed the wrought iron knocker, rapping it against the massive wooden door. They waited some time before they heard the latch release. The door opened just enough to reveal a stooped, grey haired woman.

"You must be Bredon and you the daughter," she said, eyeing Mavie with a scowl. "I am Gytha. Fordón said you would come. There is a pen behind the house for the pony. When you return, I will show you to your room. Fordón has arranged to take his meal on the courtyard by the lake. You may join him after you are settled."

"Thank you," said Bredon. "Mavie will wait here while I get our belongings and tend to the pony."

Gytha stepped to the side and motioned for Mavie to enter. Once she was inside, Gytha drew up close to Mavie, examining her face. "You are pleasing to the eye. Be careful. Fordón has a lust for youthful beauty, as you will soon see."

"Forewarned is forearmed," replied Mavie. "But know this, I am not one to be trifled with."

"Of that I have no doubt. Ring the bell when your father returns." Gytha motioned to a bell pull behind Mavie, then limped away, fading into the shadows.

Mavie stood in the doorway and looked across the courtyard to the lake beyond. The courtyard was empty and Ula's rock was too far away for Mavie's human eyes to discern if she was still there. Mavie ran her finger across the face of the door

113

while she waited. Despite its polished appearance, the surface felt rough and cracked. She was just about to check the carved stone when Bredon walked around the corner of the house with their belongings tucked under his arms. She stepped back into the house as he climbed the steps.

Bredon followed her. "Where's Gytha?"

"Gone off in the back somewhere," replied Mavie. She tugged on the bell pull. "She warned me about Fordón."

"Oh?"

"Seems he lusts after young women."

"Well, you already knew that."

Gytha appeared. She ushered them down a dark hallway to a shabby room with two straw ticks on the floor. She left them standing in the dark saying, "You will find Fordón in the courtyard. I am off to fetch supper.

"Hamor provided better than this," said Mavie. "I think this mansion house is another of Fordón's illusions."

"I agree," said Bredon, placing the bundles on the floor. "It's time to find out what he wants."

When they stepped out of the house, they saw Fordón sitting at a table under the oak tree. As they approached, he whistled. They heard a splash in the distance.

Mavie tugged on Bredon's sleeve. "Ula," she whispered.

"Patience, don't show our hand yet," said Bredon.

Fordón remained seated when they reached the table. He was wearing the same black cloak as the last time they met. The hood, however, was pulled back. The skin of his long face was smooth and dark. His black eyes were fixed on Mavie. "Be seated," Fordón said, his thin pale lips barely moving. "Perhaps your daughter would pour us some ale."

"My name is Mavie, sir." She looked at Bredon. He nodded toward the flagon. Frowning, Mavie picked it up and began to fill the tankards.

"Bredon, I am surprised this one is not yet married. She is ripe for the plucking."

"Truth be told," offered Bredon, resting his hand on Mavie's arm, "most men find her a bit trying." He paused, looking Fordón in the eye. "I did not come here to discuss my daughter."

"Of course. Swords and such, wasn't it?" Fordón said, deflecting Bredon's comment. There was a rustle in the water where the courtyard steps met the lake. They looked up to see Ula emerge from the lake. Her long hair wrapped around her body like seaweed. The water trickling down her body glistened in the afternoon sunlight. "Ah, and this is Ula," he said. "Aren't you going to greet our guests?"

"Good day to you and welcome to this table," she said, bowing her head.

"I had Gytha bring you a covering," Fordón said, holding out a folded white garment. Ula took the linen shift and slipped it over her head, carefully pulling her long hair out from the neck opening. Her wet tresses fell almost to the ground. The linen clung to her bare skin, soaking up the water. She joined them at the main table.

"Beautiful, isn't she," said Fordón. "She was a bit trying also, but not anymore."

Gytha showed up carrying a large platter and a kettle. She laid out thick trenchers of brown bread, then ladled them with mutton pottage. Without saying anything else, Fordón picked up his fork, speared a chunk of meat and stuffed it into his mouth.

They finished eating as the last light of the day faded away. Gytha reappeared to clear the table. Without warning, Fordón said, "Ula, to your room. Bredon and I have business to discuss."

Ula stood up and said, "I bid you good evening." She followed Gytha into the house.

Mavie addressed Fordón. "Thank you for this fine meal. My father and I have had a long walk this day and I am feeling tired. With your leave, I will go to my bed."

"Why, of course," said Fordón.

"Good night," said Bredon.

"Don't tell me you forgot your goodnight kiss, Father," said Mavie, throwing her arms around Bredon. She made sure the back of her head was all Fordón could see as she quickly kissed Bredon full on the lips. Before he could react, she let go of him and hurried off toward the house.

"She's an affectionate child," Bredon sputtered.

Gytha returned with two lanterns, which she placed on the table. "I prefer to discuss my business here," said Fordón, "away from any distractions."

"I'm afraid you won't be able to see the quality of my blades in this light," said Bredon.

"It is not blades I am interested in!" growled Fordón.

"Then what?"

"You have seen Ula. Do you know she is a Merin?"

"I knew as soon as I saw her! Do you forget I am a mage?"

"No! I see your tattooed eye. Ula is most beautiful and I would have her as my wife. However, even though she has taken human form, she remains a creature of the sea, cold to the touch and cold in her heart. What I seek is a spell or a charm that would make her just a little more human, so she could be a comfort in my bed. I would pay good money for such a spell."

"Spells are not to be sold like fish at the market."

"What is it to you?" asked Fordón. "Are you not the one who has abandoned his magic?"

"I prefer to make blades than to practice magic. That doesn't mean I've abandoned it. Magic is a dangerous pursuit. It can result in unexpected consequences when used by a pretender."

"I may not have a tattooed eye, but I am not new to the use of spells."

"So I have surmised," said Bredon.

"Enough of this jesting. I invited you here to do business. Now that you've feigned indignation, what is it you want?"

"Ah, Fordón, you are a shrewd business man, indeed," said Bredon. "There's no fooling you. As for what I want, I have no need of money. What have you to trade?"

"I have many things that may interest you, what is it you seek?"

"A Merin's skin, perhaps. They are a rare commodity. You should have one hidden around here."

"On the contrary," replied Fordón. "I quickly realized Ula could sense its presence. I considered it a distraction, so I destroyed it. Unfortunately, I couldn't foresee that you would want it. Otherwise, I would have kept it."

"Unfortunate indeed," said Bredon, "what else do you have that would entice me? We may yet strike a bargain."

***

It was well into the night when Bredon returned to their tiny room. Moonlight fought its way through the grimy window, dimly illuminating the room in mottled blue light. He knelt by Mavie, gently shaking her shoulder. She roused from her sleep.

"Fordón wasn't interested in blades," said Bredon, "He has proposed a barter with me in exchange for a spell. I told him I would consider his offer and inform him of my decision in the morning."

"A spell for what?"

"A spell to make Ula more human."

117

"Surely, you wouldn't!" hissed Mavie. "She doesn't need to be more human, she needs to find her sealskin and escape this monster."

"I know this is not what you want to hear," Bredon whispered. "But Ula was right. Fordón has destroyed her sealskin."

"Then she is doomed to a life of misery," groaned Mavie.

"Perhaps not. If she chooses, there is a way Ula can be free, though it comes at a price. I will explain. Then I need you to become a little mouse and go to her to find out if she is willing to pay it."

***

In the morning, Bredon and Mavie found Fordón waiting at the table in the courtyard. When they reached the table he asked, "Have made your decision?"

"Have you brought it?" asked Bredon.

Fordón reached down, retrieved a bundle and placed on the table. "As promised."

"I would have a look, if you please."

Fordón nodded in agreement. Bredon slid the bundle to the side of the table and loosened the leather ties. He peeled back the woolen cloth to reveal a sword broken an arm's length above the hilt. He held it up, sunlight reflecting off its polished surface. He held it close to his eye, examining the patterns in the blade. He showed it to Mavie. "Kellan's sword, made of elven steel by his own hand."

"Have we a bargain?" asked Fordón. Bredon looked at Mavie.

"Yes," she said.

"Yes! Yes, indeed!" cackled Fordón. He jumped up from his chair, wringing his hands and wagging his head. He grabbed Bredon's arm. "Tell me words, tell me what to say."

"Calm down,' said Bredon, wresting his arm from Fordón's grasp, "lest you make a mistake."

Fordón withdrew his hand and regained his composure. "Forgive me. You are right, of course." He looked toward the lake and whistled. "While we wait for Ula, you will prepare me."

Bredon reached into his tunic and withdrew a swatch of parchment. "The spell is complicated. I have written it down. Perhaps you would rather read it than try to commit it to memory." Fordón reached for it. Bredon drew it back. "I'll hold onto this until everything is ready. You can read the spell only one time. If you stop or make a mistake while reading it, the spell will be corrupted. And it will work best if only she hears you speak the words."

Fordón glared at Bredon. "Where is that blasted girl?" he muttered. He snatched up the sword from the table. "I'll hold onto *this* until everything is completed!" A few moments later, Ula walked up the steps, radiant in the morning sun. "Stay there," he ordered. He held out his free hand to Bredon. "I'll have that parchment now."

"And the sword?" asked Bredon.

"When I'm sure the spell works."

"Let him have it," said Mavie to Bredon. "The sooner this is over, the better."

"Your daughter is right, bladesmith. The sooner this is over, the better for all concerned."

Bredon dropped the parchment into Fordón's waiting hand. "Remember what I said. You have one chance to get it right."

"Don't worry." He sneered. He rushed over to Ula. "I am going to read something to you. I want you to pay attention." He dropped the sword to the ground. Leaning in close to her ear, he began to read from the parchment in a hushed voice.

Mavie watched, fighting back tears. "I would that it had not come to this," she said to Bredon. "Are you sure there is no other way?"

"None that is better for Ula. At least she will be free."

"And what of Fordón?"

"In the end, he will get what he bargained for."

Fordón finished reading the spell, then said, "From this moment, you will never again long for the sea." He grasped her arm, feeling a hint of warmth. "It's working. Soon you will be human."

Ula looked at Mavie, calling out, "I feel it! Remember your promise." A single tear welled in her eye, then trickled down her cheek. She touched it with her finger, then brought the tear to her lips, tasting its saltiness. In the next instant, she turned to stone, gleaming in the sun like a marble statue.

"What is this?" cried Fordón, He let go of her arm, but not before cold searing pain shot up his arm. "You did this, magician!" he screamed, lurching toward Bredon. Mid-step, his body solidified into a hideous gargoyle. It crashed to the ground, scattering shards of rock across the courtyard.

"What happened to Fordón?" Mavie gasped. "I knew Ula's fate, but did you know this would happen to him?"

"He was touching her arm when she turned. I told him Magic was a dangerous pursuit and that it could result in unexpected consequences." They slowly walked over to Ula's remains. Mavie began to cry. "I'm sorry Mavie," said Bredon.

"Look, she is smiling," Mavie said, wiping tears from her face.

"What shall we do with her?" asked Bredon.

"I promised to take her to the coast and find her a spot, away from prying eyes, where she can look out on the sea," said Mavie. "Then I will find the Merin and sing her song."

GONE FISHIN'[10]

Geedad says there was big towers right up the river a ways. Just above the bend. You can see where they was from the top of the bluff. Geedad can't though, he's blind now. He said he seen 'em when he was a little boy and they was somethin' else. But then, they got blowed up. Now, they's just a rottin' pile of rubble.

The leaves is coming out and the river is fillin' up. Geedad says the snow up in the hills is meltin' and that makes the river come up. I don't really understand how that goes, but if Geedad says it, it's good enough for me. Dad give me the mornin' off to go fishin' with Geedad.

Fount a book once while I was out gatherin' with Dad. It had lots of pictures in it. Ma called it a story book. She said the pictures was called drawin's. Below the pictures was what she called words, 'cept they weren't spoke words, but they was drawed words. She's teachin' me to read them drawed words, at least them she knows. There was this picture that showed a big ol' house with these round lookin' rooms that come up out of the roof into the sky. Ma said it was called a 'cassal'. I asked her if the towers Geedad talked about was a 'cassal'. She said she didn't think so.

Where we lives is called Nomenslan. Other folks don't come up this way hardly ever. Dad says that's good, cause it means they ain't nobody else gatherin' round here and that means more for us. I been helpin' Dad gather ever since he fount out I could see things far away so good. We goes out and I'll climb up a tree or run to the top of a hill and look for some good gatherins.

Old buildings and houses is the best for gatherin'. Next is cars and trucks. Dad says to keep an eye out for 'lectrics and such

---

[10] "Gone Fishin'" appeared on line in *The Free Library Of The Interned Void,* 8/14/2018.

cause they's good barter down river. Metal is good too, if it's the right kind. Copper and 'lumanum' is what he says to look for. He said there is this stuff called 'goad' but it's very hard to find. He said they had some a long time ago, but it went to barter. I asked Dad if I could go with him to barter. He said it was best for me to stay home to take care of Ma and Geedad instead.

Ma don't never go to barter. She stays around home and tends to the garden and cooks. She is sad most of the time. The only time she smiles is when I ask her to teach me about them drawed words. I tell her it'll come in handy when I'm big enough to go to barter. But she'll say that ain't no place for me, then put her arms around me and start to cry.

Geedad asks me to go in and find him a fish. I slip off my clothes and wade out into the water. Don't make sense to get my clothes wet and then have to wear them while they dry out. The ice has melted. The water is sure 'nuff cold, but I don't mind. Geedad needs me to find a fish, and somethin' other than varmint and taters would taste purdy good.

Geedad drives a stake in the river bank and ties one end of the heavy line to it. The other is tied to my gig. He calls it my harpoon. Said that's the way old time 'saylers' used to catch these big ol' fish called 'wales'. He said they was so big, if they was in the river, their backs would stick out of the water. I asked him how they swam around and he said they didn't live in the river but some place called the 'see'.

Geedad said he was just a little boy when some powerful bad folks called 'terrerists' blowed up the towers. He said it weren't just the ones in Nomenslan, but they done ever one in the whole world. I asked him why they'd do something like that. He said they was just plain crazy. After they done that, there was a war that lasted just one day and most everything else got blowed up. He said things got real bad after that. They was lots of fightin' and killin'. He said there come a new clear winter, but most places were too hot to live in. I don't understand how it could be hot in winter, but if Geedad says it, it's good enough for me. He said that's when his eyes got ruint.

So in the water I goes. Got to make sure I don't get tangled up in the line. The water is purdy clear. Most fish in the river are awful small, so I keep lookin'. You find the catfish out in the middle where it's deepest. That's what I'm after. I'll stay under as long as it takes. I keep swimmin' till I come up on one restin' in the mud. Good thing, cause I'm almost out of line. It ain't no wale, but it's bigger'n me. It's got two tails, split almost up to his head. Geedad says they's hard to skin when they got two tails, but the way I sees it, there's twice as much meat. I stick the gig right in behind its head and it begins to twist all around somethin' fierce. I wait until I'm sure the gig is gonna hold before I come up and swim back to shore. We'll let it go on fightin' till it's all wore out before we haul it in.

I crawl up on the shore. The air hisses through my gills as I take a gulp of air. It's awful cold sitting naked on the rocks waitin' to dry off. Anyway we won't be eatin' no varmint tonight.

THE GUY WHO WAS SEEING MONSTERS[11]

Despite being a medical professional, James Ivers still felt uneasy descending the steps into the basement housing the county morgue. He had worked with cadavers in med school, but the idea of dead bodies stored in musty lockers in the bowels of the old building was unsettling. He walked along the dim corridor until he found himself in front of a door marked 'CORONER'. He knocked.

"Come in."

Ivers pushed the door open. Inside, he found a man sitting behind an ancient metal desk.

"Dr. Ivers, I'm Ron Orbin, County Coroner," the man said, rising and extending an open hand. "Please call me Ron."

"Glad to meet you, Dr. Orbin, though not under these circumstances. Call me Jim," the young ophthalmologist responded, pumping the extended hand of the gray haired man. "You practice at the hospital, don't you?"

"Well, a qualified yes, at the Outcare Clinic. In my spare time, I serve as Coroner. One of the perks is this luxurious office suite," he laughed, sweeping his arm in a grand arc, "that the County provides in the basement along with the corpses. I especially enjoy the odor of mildew. Anyway, this is where I conduct my business. You're with Advantage Eye Institute."

"Yes, I'm down here three days a week and in Samsonville the other two. They call it an institute, but it's really just a regular ophthalmology practice."

---

[11] "The Guy Who Was Seeing Monsters" was selected to appear on Halloween in the online publication *CommuterLit - Fiction On The Go*, 10/31/2017.

"As I said, this is where I conduct my coroner business." He gestured toward a well-worn straight back chair, "Please, have a seat. I'm preparing my investigator's narrative on the findings in the death of Mr. Allen Mind. My understanding is that he visited you for an eye ailment in the days preceding his death. I want to gain some understanding as to the nature of his complaint and the medical treatment you provided."

"Yeah, the guy who was seeing monsters. I figured that's why you asked me here today. I'll be happy to do whatever I can. This sure is an unfortunate situation. You know, I've never had a patient claim he was seeing monsters, then die. Kinda creepy. I didn't administer any treatment as such. All I did was examine him and issue a diagnosis. There was no treatment called for. He was in bad shape the last time I spoke with him, going on about monsters and all, but I didn't think he'd end up dead. Have you determined the cause? I hope there's no issue with my diagnosis."

"First things first," Orbin responded. He returned to his seat behind the scuffed, grey-green metal desk. "I asked you here so I can fill in some of Mr. Mind's death history before I submit my final report. Let me assure you, this isn't about anything you did. I was really hoping you could help me understand what was going on with Mr. Mind in the days before his death – physically, mentally and perhaps spiritually. It may help me with my final report."

Ivers wrinkled his brow. "Sure, whatever I can do. I don't know if I understand what you want, but I'll give it a try."

"You did say he was seeing monsters, didn't you?"

"Well, that's what he was babbling about. You think that had any bearing on his death? Do you think he committed suicide?"

"I don't know what I think, but perhaps you can provide some information or insight that may help. That's all I can ask."

Orbin pulled open a drawer and retrieved a file folder. The two sat in silence for a moment as he thumbed through the contents. Suddenly the pipes which ran along the ceiling of the cramped office rattled violently, startling Ivers. "Don't worry, it's not the dead trying to get out." Orbin laughed. "Someone just flushed upstairs. Scared the crap out of me the first time I was in here by myself. The hospital records show that Mr. Mind came to the ER on the Friday a week before last. Says here, he complained that he was having trouble with the vision in his left eye. A blind spot that had suddenly appeared. I'm just paraphrasing, you know. The report goes on to state the ER physician, a Dr. Newton, performed an examination and issued a preliminary diagnosis of vitreous hemorrhage, recommending a visit to an ophthalmologist with thirty six hours. Advantage Eye Institute provides the on-call for eye related needs for the hospital, doesn't it?"

"Yes," Ivers responded, "In fact, Dr. Newton called that day to discuss his diagnosis."

"What happened?"

"I told him without examining Mr. Mind myself, I couldn't confirm or dispute the diagnosis. My recommendation was for the patient to see his eye doctor within the next day or so."

"Was that the extent of the conversation?"

"That was it for the first call, but Dr. Newton called back to relate that Mr. Mind did not have an eye doctor or even a personal physician in the area and asked if Mr. Mind could visit the Institute. I told him to have Mind come by after lunch, and we'd work him in. That was it, as far as talking with Dr. Newton."

Orbin picked up a pen and began writing on the paper in front of him. "Did Dr. Newton mention anything about Mr. Mind seeing monsters?"

"No."

"I assume Mr. Mind kept his appointment."

"Yes he did." Ivers leaned forward, waiting for Orbin to finish.

"Go on, I'm listening."

"OK. As I said, Mind came in that afternoon. He appeared to be a normal middle-aged man in general good health. Never had an inkling during his first visit of what was to follow. Anyway, I conducted a complete examination. I determined it to be central serous retinopathy. I told Mind it didn't require treatment and should resolve itself within 2 to 3 months. He seemed comfortable with the diagnosis and we established a follow-up visit in 3 months."

Orbin put his pen down. "I've heard of that, but never had any real experience with it. I believe it's caused by a buildup of fluid behind the retina, like a blister. Results in a blind spot?"

"Yeah. Fortunately, if you have two eyes, which most of us do, the unaffected eye will compensate, so you can have near normal vision. That's what I told Mind."

"And he bought it?"

"I thought he did."

"Did he say anything about monsters?"

"Not during this visit."

Orbin thumbed through the folder. He drew out a sheet of paper and studied it. "On the Wednesday following his visit with you, Mr. Mind was admitted to the hospital. You were called to the hospital to treat Mr. Mind. The report goes on to say…"

"That's correct," Ivers interrupted, "but I had seen Mind again in my office before that day."

"Which day?"

"Wednesday, when he went to the hospital."

"I was unaware of that. Tell me what happened," Orbin said, leaning forward.

"Well, that was on Monday. After lunch, the receptionist came back to the examination area to tell me that Mind was up front, very agitated, demanding to see me right away. I asked her to tell him I would get to him as soon as I could, but to explain I would have to see scheduled patients first. She came right back and said he was very upset and begging to be seen right away."

"What happened?"

"I went out to the waiting area and Mind was obviously upset. I decided to park him in an exam room in hopes that he would calm down."

"Did he?"

"Once he got in the room, he quieted down, but he was so upset, I decided to hear him out right then. That's when things got squirrelly."

"Squirrelly?"

"I don't know what else to call it. He said his blind spot had changed color. Said the blur had turned from grey to dull red. Said that spot had been a dead space as far as seeing anything, but now, he could see two eyes within it. He was definitely upset, pleading with me to do something. He said those eyes belonged to a monster. Looking back, I don't think I recognized just how disturbed he was."

"That was the first time he talked of a monster?"

"As far as I know."

Orbin looked up from his notes. "Did you examine him?"

Ivers drew in a breath. "Of course I did. I couldn't see any change. I told him over time, it was possible small portions of the blind spot might regenerate explaining both the color and the dots of light. I said it could look like eyes. That's when he got angry. Said I didn't understand. He said the spot was getting bigger and that the monster was looking at him. He said it was trying to get into his brain. It was obvious he was in a bad place, but I had no idea how it was going to end up. I tried to reassure him, and after a while, I thought I had him convinced there wasn't anything in his eye and in time he would see some improvement. He left and I didn't see him again until Wednesday."

Orbin raised an eyebrow. "I see. It's hard to know."

"Know what?"

"I once had a patient..." Orbin paused, placing his paperwork down, "who came in after returning from her dream Amazon rainforest vacation. Apparently she and her husband did everything – kayaking in tributaries, jungle trekking and the like. It wasn't long after they returned that she began to experience abdominal cramps, bloating, fatigue, headaches and the like. An otherwise health woman in her mid to late 40's, she was convinced she had contracted some exotic parasite and insisted I treat her for that. In fact, she got quite belligerent. As it turned out, she was pregnant. But, it wasn't until the test came back positive that she would give up on the belief she had some parasite eating away at her.

"If you practice long enough, it's inevitable you will encounter those patients who can't or won't accept what you tell them because they have absolute belief in their own self-diagnosis. They can be terribly difficult to work with. The mind controls everything in the body. A stressed-out patient can sometimes create symptoms to fit their self-diagnosis. I wouldn't be too hard on myself if I were you. Besides, I don't know if there was anything else you could have done for Mr. Mind."

"What do you mean?"

"Oh I don't know," Orbin mused. "Anything to add about Monday?"

"No, other than I never had the faintest notion about what happened on Wednesday," Ivers added, shaking his head.

"Speaking of Wednesday, let's move on."

"Sure."

"The report from the hospital states that Mind came to the ER about 10:00 AM presenting a severe wound to his left eye. After a preliminary examination, you were called."

"Well, they called the Institute and as I was the physician on site, I responded. I don't think they asked for me by name."

"Go on."

"My receptionist took the call. She said they had a patient in the ER with an eye wound and needed someone to come right away. I headed right over, no idea what I was in for. When I arrived, they took me right in and there was Mind. You could have knocked me over with a feather. He was the last person I expected to see. He had a catastrophic wound to his left eye. He was unusually calm for an individual who had experienced such trauma. There was significant damage to the cornea, sclera, and orbital muscles – really all the structures of the eye. I asked him how this had happened.

"What he said still chills me to the bone. He told me the spot in his eye had grown. As it grew, he could see the monster. He said the thing had ragged teeth and was gnawing at the edges of the spot, ripping away his sight. At some point the spot got big enough for the creature to push its head through. Mind said all he could see at that point were its teeth gnashing, straining to reach him. Mind said he knew the thing was hungry, hungry for flesh. It was then, Mind said, he had used a steak knife to gouge his eye out. Ghastly, absolutely ghastly."

"What then?"

"He was taken up to surgery where what remained of his eye was removed. Fortunately, Mind had not damaged the tissue behind the eye and the result was a normal enucleation with no complications. Prognosis was for a normal recovery. Post op, he was taken to the psychiatric ward for evaluation."

"Yes, that is consistent with the report from the hospital. When did you next see Mr. Mind?"

"I stopped by the next morning, before I headed to Samsonville."

"And what was Mind's condition at that time?"

"Pretty much what you would expect 18 to 20 hours post op. I checked his chart. Apparently he became agitated during the night, and was sedated to allow him to rest."

"Did he say anything?"

"He said something about the spot. At first I thought he was talking about his left eye, but as he went on, it became clear he was referring to his right eye."

"His right eye? Did you examine him?"

"I took a look with a direct ophthalmoscope, but it's not really the right instrument. I couldn't make a determination. It needed to be done it in the office, but that was out of the question. Given the circumstances, I thought it was probably just a delusion." Ivers paused and slumped back in his chair. "I didn't think much more of it until Friday morning when I stopped by the hospital to check on him. That's when I found out he had died. I felt bad about that. They were pretty close-lipped about it, so I really didn't find out much more other than it happened sometime in the early morning. Sad, sad business. I checked the newspaper, but it had even less information. I was hoping you could fill me in."

Orbin removed his eyeglasses and set the folder aside. "According to the report from the hospital, he started ranting Thursday afternoon. Same sort of stuff he told you. Went on about a hole in his eye, some monster trying to get in. Begged and pleaded for them to take out his other eye. He must have gone wild - so violent they had to restrain him. From the chart records, they pumped the sedatives into him. "

"They didn't overdose him did they?"

"No, no, they administered a significant amount, but not enough to kill him. I interviewed all the staff and they were all in agreement: Mind continued to struggle in a semi-conscious state for the rest of the day and into the night. By all accounts he wailed and thrashed incessantly. Even with the sedation they had administered, he had to be kept in restraints. Never stopped ranting. He went on and on about monsters eating him alive and the only way to stop it was to cut out his eye. They said he cursed, he prayed, threatened to kill them all if they didn't do it. I can't imagine the extent of his suffering. The duty nurse reported he suddenly grew quiet about 3:00 am. According to her statement, she went to check on him immediately. Data confirms the monitors were recording vital signs up to that point. She said by the time she got to his room, he was dead."

"I didn't know the man, but I'm sorry he died like that," Ivers said. "Seems like a horrible way to go. He must have had a massive heart attack or stroke to go that quickly. The stress he was under must have been too much for him."

Orbin sat back in his chair and folded his arms. "That's what I thought at first. I examined the surgical wound. Looked normal, no hemorrhage, or other abnormality detected. I checked the meds, nothing there to indicate a problem. There was nothing left to do but perform an autopsy. I can tell you he didn't die of a heart attack or stroke."

"What then."

"I don't know what to tell you, much less what to put in my report."

"I don't understand."

"Neither do I. You see, his skull was empty, his brain gone, scooped out like a Halloween pumpkin."

THE WILDFLOWER ADVENTURE

It was a bright, early summer morning that found the four young children sitting in the kitchen of the cozy stone home which sat at the top of the hill. Freshly mown fields rolled down to the creek below. Emma, Sara, and Will sat on the tall stools at the worn counter in the kitchen and looked out the window over the sink as their mother drove off to do some shopping.

"Now, mind Great Grandma and stay out of mischief," She had said, as she kissed each on the forehead. "I'll be back at three."

Alexander, their cousin, sat on his stool and busily drew brightly colored pictures with the well-worn crayons Great Grandma kept in an old cigar box.

Soon, they turned their attention to the spry old woman who was pouring glasses of fresh lemonade. While she poured, she talked with the children, asking them about dancing lessons, church, what they were doing for the summer and the like.

She placed the glasses on small hand knitted coasters; each had a different flower embroidered on its face.

"There you are! A red rose for Sara, a white tulip for Emma, a blue Iris for Will and a yellow jonquil for Alexander. Shall I bake some muffins for later?" she asked with a soft laugh, knowing the response she would receive.

"Yes!"

"Yes!"

"Yes!"

The three turned their heads to Alexander, who continued his furious drawing, oblivious to all else.

"He says yes, too!" Emma said, nodding her head.

The children watched as she pulled a big bowl from the cabinet under the sink and busied herself gathering the ingredients.

Positioning the bowl on the counter, she poured in the mix. Then she added some milk and finally picked up an egg that had been resting in the spoon carrier on the counter.

She was poised to crack it open when Emma asked, "Where do eggs come from?"

Looking up, she paused. "Well, I am an old Kansas farm girl; and I can tell you that eggs come from chickens on the farm." She held up the egg between her thumb and forefinger. "An egg is like a little house. On the farm, baby chicks grow inside until they are ready to come out, then they break the shell with their beaks. But until that, they have everything they need right inside – that is of course unless a fox steals the egg."

With that, she tapped the side of the egg on the bowl and pried the now split shell open to allow its contents to pour out. "That," she said, pointing to the bright yellow blob in the middle, "is the yolk. That's what the baby chick eats while it waits to hatch. The rest is there to help it along. The shell keeps the little chick safe until it is ready to come out."

Looking out the window, Sara watched the blades of the old weather-beaten windmill in the flower garden turn slowly.

"What makes it turn?" she asked inquisitively.

"Why, the wind my dear. You can't see it, but it is there. It moves the clouds, makes the leaves shake before a rain, and cools us with its soft breath on a sunny day."

While she stirred the ingredients in the bowl with a worn wooden spoon, she watched Will hold his hand out and wiggle his fingers in the sunlight that was spilling in through the window. A shadow of a tiny hand danced on the counter surface. As the "legs" of the shadow walked up the side of the sugar bowl, she said, "There is an old poem by Robert Louis Stevenson that goes like this:

'I have a little shadow that goes in and out with me,
And what can be the use of him is more than I can see.
He is very, very like me from the heels up to the head;
And I see him jump before me, when I jump into my bed.'"

Alexander slid down from his stool, took his latest drawing to the refrigerator and hung it there with the others. He tugged on the old woman's apron. She looked down as he pointed to the latest addition to her gallery.

"Well, Alexander what do I see?" she said, eyeing the freshly hung picture with a swath of blue crayon running from side to side. It was punctuated with small green dots perched along its upper edge.

"It's the creek, Great Grandma. And those are the frogs," he said, pointing to the green dots.

"And certainly fine frogs they are."

"May we go out and play?" asked Emma.

"Why sure, but don't go in the creek, its not made of crayons, and be careful if you go in the woods. You don't know what you may find in there."

The four bounded down the steps and out the screen door into the fresh bright sunlight. A soft breeze blew strands of hair across their cheeks.

"What shall we do?" asked Will.

"We could draw pictures on the driveway with chalk," piped up Sara.

"We could catch frogs," offered Alexander

"Oh no we couldn't!" chided Emma. "Great Grandma just told us to stay out of the creek; besides, I have a much better idea."

"What if we don't like it?"

"Well, I like it and so will Sara and since I am the oldest that means you are outvoted."

"You haven't even told us yet," Will said indignantly.

"If you will kindly be quiet, I will. I think we should go pick some wildflowers for Great Grandma. You know how she likes flowers."

"That sounds like great fun. There should be plenty down there," said Sara pointing down the hill to the woods that bordered the creek.

Alexander folded his arms. "Wait a minute, we haven't even voted."

"Alright then. All in favor of gathering some flowers for Great Grandma instead of catching nasty frogs for themselves raise their right hand. Let's see. One, Two. Looks like we pick flowers."

Will stood by glaring as Sara picked up the basket Great Grandma kept by the back door for gathering cut flowers from her garden. "This will do nicely. We won't come back until it's overflowing."

The children raced down the hill right to the edge of the woods.

"I don't see any flowers," Will said mockingly.

"You have to search for them, silly; they won't jump in the basket by themselves."

"How about these?" asked Sara, holding up two dandelions.

"I don't know," said Emma, "Great Granddad usually digs those out of the yard. Weeds, he calls them."

"Wait, did you hear that?" asked Alexander, putting one hand up and cupping the other to his ear. Sounds like... like a strange bird singing."

The girls kept chattering away, discussing whether or not to include dandelions.

"Shhhhhhh!"

They stopped their conversation and looked at Alexander. Slowly he pointed into the woods. Standing very still, they peered into the dark shadows, straining to hear.

After a moment or two, Sara said, "Doesn't sound like any bird to me. It's more like a harp."

"Sounds like a small drum to me – thrump, thrump, tumpity tump, thrump, thrump, tumpity tump," piped in Will.

"No," said Emma, who had stepped right up to a large oak tree standing at the very edge of the woods, "more like bees humming a lullaby." With that, she stepped into the shadows under the canopy of leaves.

"Don't go in there!" Sara called after her. "Remember what Great Grandma said about the woods."

"She didn't say we couldn't go in the woods," Will reminded her. "Come on, don't be a fraidy cat. What can happen?"

"Nothing!" cried Alexander

Sara watched Will dart right into shadows followed by Alexander, precisely where Emma had entered the woods. She looked back up the hill for a moment, then summoning up her courage called out, "Wait for me."

Will had followed Emma for what seemed a fair distance when he came upon her leaning against the bough of a huge sycamore. With Alexander beside him, he looked back to see Sara hurrying along. Behind her, the bright sunlit green of the grass in the fields was no longer visible. Here and there a solitary beam of sunlight drifted down through the thick layers of leaves, creating a brilliant glowing blotch on the dead leaves piled on the forest floor. Emma was looking ahead deeper into the woods. Sara came up breathing hard, more from excitement than from running after them.

"It's coming from right over there." Emma pointed straight ahead. "I can hear it clearer now. Can't you?"

Sara, Will and Alexander stood still for a moment, letting the sounds of the woods filter over them. Soon, Sara tilted her head to the right as if to give her ear more room to listen. "No," she said in a soft voice. "It's that way."

"No way, I hear it from over there," Will whispered, as he turned full to the left and pointed with his chin.

"I think it's right above us," said Alexander, looking straight up.

The children fell under the spell of the soft sounds that wrapped around them like a hug from Great Grandma when she sang them to sleep. The sweet smell of the forest filled their heads like the aroma of spiced tea. The soft leaves of the forest floor beckoned them like a warm bed at the end of a long day.

Sara looked around to see Emma sitting at the base of the tree. Her eyes were closed and her arms lay motionless in her lap. Sara tapped Will on the shoulder. He didn't respond. She grabbed his arm and gave it a gentle shake.

"Will!"

He turned, eyelids drooping. "I'm sorry, I thought I saw something."

Alexander began to sway back and forth as he gazed at the leaves above.

"Help me with Emma, Will." Worry crept into her voice. She was suddenly very sleepy. Barely able to hold her eyes open, she tugged on Will's arm as he slumped to the ground, followed immediately by Alexander.

She was dreaming of a great banquet in a huge hall girded round with tall columns, when she awoke to the vibrant sound of flutes, drums and fiddles. Will and Sara were sitting beside her in a broad clearing circled by tall trees. Alexander was lying on his back yawning and stretching. The floor of the clearing was covered in an intricate mosaic of flowers, mushrooms and different hues of grass. Directly ahead, stood a large tree. Perched atop the birch brackets circling its trunk stood four frogs. The first, wearing a bright yellow scarf, played the flute, trilling the notes with a flick of his long tongue. The second, topped with a bright blue cap, thumped a large webbed foot perfectly in time as he fluttered the beater over the bodhrán he held. The third, wearing a white jerkin, played the fiddle, the bow flying over the strings in a blur. And the fourth, sporting a wide red sash, strummed the harp, fingers dancing about the strings in a wild jig. They were accompanied by a variety of other musicians who had taken up their stations at the base of the tree. The music flowed out, enchanting the children just as the smell of fresh baked muffins floating out of an open window on a summer's day entices all who breathe in the intoxicating aroma.

All around them, dancers cavorted to the wild and capricious melody. They were a variety of shapes and sizes; but whether tall or short, stout or thin, they each moved in perfect unison. The females wore loose gowns of soft sunset hues, gathered in at the waist by a belt of gold web. Bright wildflowers were embroidered around the openings for their neck and along the sleeves. About their heads, they wore a band of brightly colored silk. Delicate sandals of silver adorned their feet. The males wore light tunics of forest colors, cinched by sturdy woolen belts, wore over loose trousers. Some wore caps and others tied their flowing hair behind their heads. They were either barefoot or wore soft leather boots. The dancers' faces were as varied as pebbles in a stream. Some were long and graceful, while others were round and plump. But all wore a gentle and warming smile.

Before the children could catch their breath, the music took on a wistful and plaintive tone and the dancers, despite their complex footwork, seemed to glide across the ground without so much as disturbing a single petal of the most delicate flower. The dancing continued for some time. The revelers never seemed to tire; and though the musicians played continually, each moment brought a new and more beautiful note that the one before. All at once, a trumpet blared. The music faded and the dancers assembled in a perfect circle. Then, several stepped back to form an opening. More trumpets rang out as a quartet of warriors in golden armor stepped solemnly into the opening. Reaching the center, they turned, and dropping to one knee, bowed to the figure entering the circle. In turn, all the dancers and musicians bowed their heads.

A herald stepped out from behind the figure announcing in a clear deep voice, "All welcome Rhoswyn Shalee, White Rose of the Fields, and Queen of the Fae." The figure reached up with long slender hands and removed the shimmering veil that covered her face.

The children gazed at her in awe. Tall and slender, the Queen was clothed in a shimmering gown of white. She wore a necklace with a brilliant sapphire as large as a robin's egg around her neck. Her russet hair, pulled back from her face, splashed over her shoulders falling to her waist. A delicate crown of gold sat atop her head.

The Queen surveyed the assemblage before her, raising her hands as she spoke, "Greetings, fair children of Fae. Your music and dance make my heart light. We shall have more before this day is over, however, we must first deal with those who have ventured into this circle without invitation."

The children huddled close together as the Queen pointed a long slender finger at them. She moved toward them, drawing so close that she seemed as tall and noble as the great trees that bound the forest clearing. She held them in her gaze for a long moment. Then she spoke.

"It is said that entering the Fairy realm is indeed a foolish thing. Those who enter sometimes do not leave. There are many

142

legends and myths concerning the Fae, some bright and others dark. All things are possible here. You are indeed fortunate that you chose this spot and not the high woods," she said, pointing to the wooded area above their Great Grandmother's house. "There, foul things roam. Even as we speak, my husband, Kellen Aelfdene, Warrior King of the Elves, travels those dark woodlands. He and his brave company of elves search for the Forgas, a wild goblin clan and their wicked leader Ziga. It is said that they have caused much mischief in those woods of late. You'll find the kind folk here much more civilized."

"Please ma'am, we didn't mean any harm," pleaded Emma. "We just wanted to pick some flowers for Great Grandmother. That's all. If it's OK with you, we'll just leave quietly the way we came in." She started to tug on Sara's arm.

"First, you arrive unannounced and uninvited, then you seek to depart without as much as a nod?" the Queen questioned, leveling her eyes directly on the children. "What would the Great Grandmother think, Emma?"

Emma stood speechless watching the Queen, who tilted her head slightly and raised an eyebrow inviting a response. Sara tucked in behind her older sister, hoping to avoid the Queen's attention. Alexander stood still and gazed up at the beautiful Queen. Finally, Will spoke up, his curiosity overcoming caution.

"Are those really frogs?" he said, pointing to the musicians across the way.

"Yes, Will, and the finest musicians in this land or any other. Is there anything else you would like to know?"

Before he could answer, Sara blurted out, "How did you know Will's name?" Surprised by the sounds coming from her mouth, she immediately covered it with her hand as if she could hide what she had just said.

"Sara, a Fairy Queen knows many things, not the least of which are the names of those who enter her home." Looking down at Alex she continued, "Am I right that your Great Grandmother lives in the stone house on the hill?"

"Yes," said Emma, finally regaining her voice.

"Yes indeed, your Great Grandmother is Vivian, she who gives life, and is much respected by our folk."

"You know Great Grandmother?"

"We know of her," said the Queen with a broad smile. Then knitting her eyebrows together as if in deep thought, she continued, "But enough of this: we must turn our attention to the matters at hand. What shall be done with the four of you? We could keep you here until our dancing is completed, but that might last for years!"

The children's eyes grew wide.

"Or, we could turn you into toadstools, but that would be no fun."

They breathed a collective a sigh of relief.

"No, I think I know just the right thing!

The dancers, who up to this moment had maintained a respectful silence, began to twitter in rapt anticipation. The Queen turned, raising her hands, "Silence please!" A hush fell over the crowd. With a wink of her eye unseen to the children, she whirled around to face them again and with a grand flourish of her hand announced, "Riddles!" The crowd erupted in applause and cheers. The children stared blankly at each other.

"Four children, four riddles," the Queen explained. "Answer all and home you go."

"Sure!" blurted out Will. Sara darted out from behind Emma, quickly covering his mouth with her hand, hoping the Queen had not heard. The crowd erupted in louder applause and more cheers.

"Wonderful," the Queen chortled.

"But, your majesty," Emma pleaded, "Don't Sara and I get to vote on this?"

"Me too," said Alexander.

"Nay, a word spoken is a word given. Remember this lesson; for once a riddle is asked, whoever speaks, speaks for all. You may give one answer and one answer only, so make sure it is the right answer. Come, let us ready for the contest."

With that, the Queen walked gracefully to the center of the clearing to a large smooth stone inlaid with silver, surrounded by a ring of wildflowers. Clapping her hands four times, a group of squat elves carried out a golden throne and gently placed it behind her on the stone. Four smaller chairs were then produced and arranged in an arc in front of the Queen. In between, a round table inlaid with silver images was placed. The onlookers gathered close around, maintaining a respectful distance between the Queen and her guests. A low murmur hovered like the drone of bees in the hive. The children stood in anticipation waiting for a sign from the Queen. She sat down and waved her hand in a wide arc for the children to take their seats. As soon as they sat down, the onlookers made themselves comfortable on the forest floor.

The Herald looked around and satisfied that all was in order, called out in his deep voice, "The challenge has been offered and accepted. Let the contest begin!"

A hush fell over the clearing; even the birds in the trees seemed to be listening. The Queen leaned forward looking at the children. Then, in a solemn voice she said:

"I'm the part of the bird that's not in the sky.
I can swim in the creek and yet remain dry.
I come out to play when the sun is bright,
But disappear in the dark of night."

The crowd twittered in anticipation of the children's answer. Emma, who had taken the center seat, looked quizzically at others as if asking what to say. Sara put her hands up to her lips and stared back at Emma with a wide eyed look of bewilderment. Emma leaned forward pushing her face closer, eyes pleading for an answer. The more she stared, the more lost Sara looked. Emma was so busy with Sara, she didn't feel Will's tugs at her sleeve until he almost pulled her out of his chair.

"A shadow," he said sheepishly. "It's a shadow."

Emma's heart pounded at the sound of Will's voice. Why had he blurted out the first silly thing that came into his head? Foolish boy, now all was lost. A hush fell over the crowd. A broad, wry smile appeared on the Queen's face. Emma gasped in a deep breath and held it waiting to hear their fate.

"Well done," the Queen said in a quiet voice, "Young Will has indeed solved the riddle." The crowd cheered and applauded. The Queen held up her hands. "The first challenge has been met and to the second we advance. But first we shall honor them in a song and dance. "

The frogs who had been patiently waiting immediately struck up a merry tune and the circle of observers began to cavort to the bright music. The children sat quietly as the revelers danced to the ebb and flow of the music. Merry voices sang along and fairy hands clapped in time with the bodhráns.

After what seemed to be quite a long time to the children, the Queen made a gesture to the Herald, who had been serenely standing at her side through the dancing and merriment. He clapped his hands four times at which the musicians stopped playing and the dancers relaxed. "Let the second challenge be offered." Silence, again overtook the crowd. The dancers sat gently down in the grass among the flowers.

The Queen spread her arms out to either side and looking up into the sky said,

"Strong enough to move a ship,
Yet right through your fingers it will slip.
Makes the mightiest trees sway.
Gently cools you on a sunny day."

This time, Emma glared right at Will. He didn't know if she wanted him to answer or if she was daring him to open his mouth. He shrugged and cocked his head, saying nothing. Emma steadied her eyes on him for a moment more before turning to Sara, who had yet to remove her hands from her lips. Alex sat next to her tracing the silver images in the table with his fingers. Emma closed her eyes, thinking for all she was worth. The lines of the riddle played over and over, but she could not think of an answer. Soon, she became aware of movement next to her. She opened her eyes to see Sara waving her hands excitedly. A smile beamed across her face. Emma watched her for a moment until she was satisfied that Sara knew the answer and gave a quick nod.

"The Wind!" she cried. "The Wind."

"Well, this one has found her voice again, and quite a voice it is for it has spoken the right answer." The Queen clapped her hands together joyfully. The crowd laughed in response. The Queen held up her hands. "The second challenge has been met and to the third we advance. But first we shall honor them with fine repast. "

Before the children had time to gasp in astonishment, the whole assembly disappeared in a frantic dash. The dust had hardly had time to settle when just as quickly and without warning they reappeared, each carrying an array of pots and platters, pitchers and plates all filled full with food of all sorts. The Herald produced a smooth linen table cloth which he flung across the table. Immediately, a service of the finest Elvin silver was placed laden with seedcakes, nuts and wild strawberries. Delicate crystal goblets were filled with sweet honeysuckle nectar. All around tables and toadstools were piled high with sumptuous fare and the assembly waited with napkins tucked.

The Queen stood up and raised her goblet. "Here's to our honored guests. So far they have passed all tests. Two more they must pass this day, before they may journey on their way. But before they face another riddle, let us pause for food and fiddle."

The fairies raised their glasses and the frog in the white jerkin drew his bow across the strings of his fiddle and the feast began. The bright tune was accompanied by laughter and the clatter of plates and cups being emptied and filled kept rhythm with the bodhrán. Emma and Sara politely nibbled at their seedcakes and delicately sipped from the goblets. Will and Alexander, on the other hand, wolfed down the contents of their plates with both hands, stopping only long enough to gulp down mouthfuls of the sweet nectar.

After the laughter subsided and the plates were emptied, the Queen made a quick motion with her hand to the Herald, who immediately waved a shimmering banner to and fro. In and instant, the pots and platters, pitchers and plates disappeared, and the dancers assembled in their ring around the Queen and the children.

The Herald rapped four times on the table with a short baton. "Let the third challenge be offered." The onlookers quietly sat down.

The Queen, still standing, looked all around, then down at the children and said:

"In a round marble hall white as milk,
Lined with skin as soft as silk.

148

Within a fountain crystal-clear,
A golden ball does appear.
No doors there are to this stronghold,
Yet thieves break in to steal its gold."

Emma looked at Sara, Will and Alex who returned blank stares. A low murmur flowed about the fairies gathered around. She then turned toward the Queen, who was examining the sapphire which hung about her neck, holding it between her thumb and forefinger just as her Great Grandma had held the egg earlier. Emma tried to think of an answer. The blank stares from the others made it clear it was up to her to solve this riddle, but she couldn't think. She watched the Queen gently holding the sapphire.

"Wait!" she cried, "I know, I know! It's... it's... it's an egg."

Silence quickly fell over the onlookers. The Queen let the sapphire fall back into place around her neck. Emma looked at the Queen confidently, a small smile stealing on her lips.

"An egg indeed," laughed the Queen. "It seems you have paid attention." The Queen bowed slightly toward Emma and then said. "The third challenge has been met and to the fourth we advance. But a fairy rade shall honor them before the last. " A mighty cheer rose up from the fairies. Of all activities, a fairy rade is the most solemn and beloved. Fairy horses were brought forth. Their bridles were silver and wildflowers were braided into their flowing manes. The fairies took to their saddles and formed a long procession behind the Queen.

The Herald helped each child in turn to mount a horse. Atop, they felt as safe and comfortable as if they were sleeping in their own cozy beds at home. The Herald led their horses to the procession until they stood two each on either side of the Queen. Her horse was pure white. She sat on a blue blanket spun from the finest spider's silk. The horse's bridle was made of gold, and red flowers adorned its mane. Finally, the Herald sprang upon his horse and the procession began to move.

The grand cavalcade moved through the woods at a leisurely pace. The only sound heard was the soft ringing of the bridle bells and the sweet mingling of fairy voices. Along the way, the forest animals bowed solemnly to the Queen. The children were amazed at the spectacle. They rode on for some time and could scarcely believe that the woods were so big that such a caravan would go unnoticed. They returned to the clearing just as the sun was about to drop behind the trees.

After all had dismounted, Emma turned toward the Queen. "We thank you for everything, but it is getting late and it is time for us to return home."

"Time is of little consequence here and besides there is one riddle left. Remember? A word spoken is a word given. Four children, four riddles." the Queen explained. "Answer all and home you go."

"But... "

"But all you have to do is answer this riddle and off you go." She nodded to the Herald who produced a bell and rang it four times. All the fairies crowded in close as the Queen intoned the last riddle.

> "What can run but never walks,
> Has a mouth but never talks,
> Has a head but never weeps,
> Has a bed but never sleeps?"

The children suddenly felt very tired. They had been gone far too long and would never be able to explain all this to Great Grandma who they knew would be very worried and very upset.

They slumped in their chairs and looked at each other hoping one of them knew the answer. Alexander looked down at the silver images in the table. They reminded him of the picture he had drawn for Great Grandma. He ran his finger along the long silver band that flowed across the table. He looked closer at the small green dots that lay along either side. Frogs! They were frogs. Then the long silver band must be the Creek.

Before he realized it, he had blurted out, "It's the creek, the creek, right there! Just like in my picture." Realizing what he had done, he slapped both hands across his mouth as if to hold the words in. Silence hovered over the clearing.

The Queen stood up, holding her arms outstretched over the children. They held their breath waiting. "Four children – four riddles," the Queen proclaimed. "Answered all and home they shall go." A mighty cheer rose from the fairies, who by now had come so close that the children could have hugged them from sheer relief and happiness.

"Before you go, I have a gift for you," the Queen said. "It is that which you desire." She clapped her hands four times and the Herald brought out a small chest and placed it on the table. The Queen opened the chest and reached in retrieving a diamond, a ruby, a sapphire, and a small bar of gold. The rays of the sun, dropping behind the trees glistened, off the gems and gold, lighting the clearing with a warm glow. Then without warning, she threw the treasure high in the air to catch the full rays of the sun. A blinding light filled the clearing and a thunder clap boomed through the woods.

Emma opened her eyes to see Sara, Will and Alex lying on soft leaves nearby. They were just starting to wake up, stretching and rubbing their eyes. It was a moment before anyone could say anything.

"Does anyone remember about going in the forest?" Emma asked tentatively.

"About frogs?" asked Will.

"About fiddles?" asked Alexander.

"About fairies?" asked Sara.

"Yes, about them all!" cried Emma. "And the riddles, the dancing, the feast and the rade?

"Yes!"

"Yes!"

"Yes!"

"Then it must be true. We were really there." cried Emma excitedly. Then thinking of how late it must be, she said, "Hurry, we must get back to Great Grandma's." And with that, she started to run out of the woods.

"Wait!" said Alexander. "What about the treasure?"

"The treasure, of course," cried Will.

"We almost forgot," added Emma.

The children looked around. They were not in the clearing. In fact, they were just inside the edge of the woods. They searched for the chest and the treasure but it was nowhere to be seen. They did, however, find the basket filled overflowing with wildflowers – red, yellow, white and blue. They looked at each other and agreed that the basket had been empty when they had entered. In the end, they decided it was some fairy mischief and left the woods for the journey back up the hill to Great Grandma's house.

They were tired, thirsty and hungry when they reached the cozy house at the top of the hill. Emma burst through the door. Great Grandma was placing a baking tin in the oven.

"We're sorry we're late," she said breathlessly.

"Late?" said Great Grandma, looking up at the clock over the sink. "You've only been gone ten minutes."

"That can't be!" added Sara, who had just climbed up the steps.

"No," said Will, as he came in the door. "We went on a fairy rade."

"Hold on just a minute," Great Grandma said, looking at the three bedraggled children. "Where's Alexander?"

"Right here. You all forgot the basket with the flowers," he said, looking at Emma, Sara and Will. "I had to go back and get it."

"Great Grandma, we met a fairy queen, and she made us guess riddles." explained Emma.

"And she gave us some treasure too, but then she took it back," said Alexander, as he handed her the basket brimming with flowers.

Great Grandma looked at the basket and smiled. "Wildflowers are Nature's treasures. And it looks like you hit the jackpot."

"Well we did go looking for wildflowers for you, Great Grandma," said Sara.

"Yeah, and the queen did say she was going to give us what we desired," added Will.

"Did you remember to thank the Queen for her hospitality?" asked Great Grandma.

The children shook their heads no.

"Well, next time I speak with Queen Rhoswyn Shalee, I will thank her for you. Now go get cleaned up."

NOT ALL THE WAY DEAD

I know I ain't dead. At least I think, not all the way dead. The way I see it, if I was all the way dead, I'd be settled in somewhere by now, one place or the other. Heaven or Hell. Anyway, I wouldn't be here. Can't be thinking about that right now. I got some things that needs to be done. Things that won't let me move on. You see, I've got scores to settle before I can be dead.

In the evening when it's whispering time, the old folks tell the children to keep away from the dark places when the shadows creep out from their hiding places. Cause, that's where them that don't know they's dead, will be lurkin'. Don't get me wrong. I'd rather be all the way dead so's I could move on. Just cause you's buried, and the worms are coming for their meal, don't mean you's all the way dead. Not if you got unfinished business. That's the way it is with me. I can't be leaving with things undone. Won't be leavin' till all is set straight.

I don't rightfully know who it was that stabbed me. Didn't know their names. Didn't know their faces. I was minding my own business. Going home. Just had me a taste down at Ruben's. It was payday and I had me a pocket full of money. Not just jingling money, but folding money. Whoever it was, they was waitin' for me in the night. Yes, there under the new moon, in the pitch black, where cowards and murderers does their work. I had just come out of Rubin's and turned up the alley, shortcuttin' to my house, when they come out of nowhere and beat me and stabbed me till I couldn't fight no more. They took my money and Daddy's gold watch, then left me with my life oozing out in the mud. I didn't see who they was, but I come to know them just before everythin' went black.

There was three of them. Two to beat me and one to cut me. I've already found the ones who beat me. I'm sure they are all the way dead, cause after I was done with each one, the black creatures come up from down below. They seeped out of the shadows and cracks, snatching up their souls, dragging them down into the fire. That leaves the one who cut me. Once I'm done with him, I can be all the way dead. Maybe then, I can move on. But not before.

The old folk say them that don't know they is dead are powerful dangerous. They're right on that account. See, I'm powerful dangerous. I got my ways of making things right. When I finds that last one, the one that dragged his blade across my throat, I'll reach right inside him and grab hold of this heart, squeezin' nice an slow 'till it can't beat no more. Then, I'll blow an icy breath into his soul to cool him off one last time before the black creatures drags him down. Down through the black so far he can't see where he come from. Down into the burning.

So here I am, and here I'll stay, searching in the dark places when the shadows grow long, cause that's where murderers and cowards walk. That's where I'll be waiting for him, the last one. I'll know him when he comes, cause I remember the ragged sound of his murdering blood coursing through his veins. I remember the foul smell of his evil thoughts rotting in his brain. I remember the scorching heat of his sins burning in his soul. Don't matter how long it takes, I'll keep waiting. I got time.

And after it's done and the black creatures has taken him away, maybe they'll come back and take me down. Maybe not. Don't matter. Can't be thinking about that right now. I got a score to settle before I can be dead.

SIGAFORGAS[12]

Of all I have read or heard, I can remember little to quote save for the lines of a poem I first heard as a child.

> Late in the night
> When the moon shines bright
> And the bullfrogs silently frown,
> You'll find that you oughter
> Not be by the water
> Lest you be grabbed and pulled right down.

It's not a widely known poem. In fact, I don't think anyone has ever heard it outside of Fern Creek. It makes no matter though. If you grew up there, you understand.

I first heard it when I was 4 or 5 and old enough to go outside on my own and play. Back then, most folks didn't live all crowded together in subdivisions that stretched for miles and miles around the shopping mall. Like us, they lived either in town or out in the rural areas. We lived on a few acres my grandparents had bought tucked in among some farms. Grandmother and Grandfather lived down the hill and my Aunt, Uncle and cousins lived over the hill. It was that simple. We had woods and a creek as good as any park. Now if you grew up in such a setting, there's no need to say any thing else. If you didn't, then there's no way to explain how that could be so much better than sitting at the computer or hanging around the mall as kids do today.

As with most legends and tales, the poem was part entertainment and part lesson. All of us were allowed free reign to

---

[12] Sigaforgas appeared in *Neo-Legends to Last a Deathtime,* an anthology, published by KY Story, 2015.

explore and play anywhere on the property. Moreover, of all the things there were to do, the creek was always a favorite place. Looking back, I can see the dangers inherent for children playing there. Nevertheless, we were oblivious then and despite the best efforts of our parents and grandparents we paid little attention to their pleas to be careful and stay out of the creek. However, the poem, however fun to hear, had its affect on our willingness to play in the creek after dark.

Many's the child
Feeling free and wild
Who tested this tale with no fear.
The last they were seen
Was down by the stream
When they would suddenly disappear.

Of course, as I grew older and more skeptical of such tales spun by grown-ups, the less I thought I believed there was anything in the creek that was a danger to me. However, I was never quite able to dismiss a nagging fear that something nasty might just be in there.

One hot, summer day, I was walking up Watterson Trail to the corner to buy a soda. I had just crossed the high bridge over Fern Creek, busily kicking an Oertle's 92 bottle cap along the blacktop. The object was to keep it between the white line on the edge of the road and the tar that had oozed to the surface. The tar would stick to your sneakers if you were dumb enough to step in it and would surely grab the bottle cap if you weren't careful.

I was so deep in concentration; I almost swallowed my gum when I heard:

"Boy, how'd you like to make two dollars?"

I looked up and found myself face to face with an old woman standing by a battered mailbox. Another foot and I would have bumped right into her.

"I dunno. What've I got to do?" Looking at the tall shaggy grass in the yard, I could guess what it was.

"Come this way," she said as she stepped back in the yard and headed toward the old house that stood up the bank from the creek, "the tools are around back." I hesitated for a moment and then followed her along the side of the house across the yard to a shaky old shed.

"You'll find what you need in here," she said pulling open the creaky door. Spiders scurried into the shadows and dust sparkled in the sunlight against the dark opening. "Mow the lawn between here and the fence and rake up the clippings. You can dump them on the brush pile in the back. When you're done with that, pull up the cattails along the creek and pitch them on the pile. I need a clear view of the creek."

I'd seen this house every time I had passed this way, but I really hadn't paid much attention to it. Never had seen any sign that anyone lived there. The yard always seemed untended. Never saw a car in the drive or a light on in the window. Until that moment, it hadn't dawned on me that the same Fern Creek that flowed along my yard also flowed along her yard. Of course, many things hadn't dawned on me back then.

"Be careful down by the creek," she said with a wry smile, "don't let Sigaforgas get you."

Remember how you felt when you almost fell out of a tree or got caught reading a comic book in school? That's what I felt. I had never heard anyone else outside my family ever say that name and it startled me to hear her say it.

Now I'll be heard

159

And you'll be assured
Of the name that should abhor us.
Your blood'll run cold
For the name to be told
Is none other than Sigaforgas!

I don't know if she could see it, but my face got hot and I felt like running home. Instead, I stood there for a moment and stared at her.

"Oh, there's others than your folks that know about the Sigaforgas."

"That's just a story they use to scare little kids. Only babies are scared to go down by the creek," I said, hoping my voice wouldn't betray my anxiety.

"Then the cattails are doomed. If you get thirsty, use the hose by the back door. I'll call you for lunch." With that, she turned and left.

I made quick work of the mowing the small yard. It wasn't really a morning's work, but at noon, I was still wandering around the yard gathering up tiny bits of flotsam and jetsam to toss on the pile. I had avoided looking at the cattails. I was still a little ashamed that the old woman's mention of you-know-what flustered me so. In addition, the thought of standing in the muck and mire to pull out the cattails gave me the willies. This was silly of course, because if I had been at home, more than likely I'd have been playing in the same creek. None-the-less, I kept myself busy in the yard until she called for lunch.

We sat on the porch in old wicker chairs. The curtains at the windows floated in and out with the breeze as if the house was slowly breathing. She had fixed peanut butter and sweet pickle sandwiches served with ice tea in tall glasses. I didn't say anything as I ate my sandwich watching the water drip down the side of the glass.

"I see you haven't started on those cattails yet." She said matter-of-factly.

I looked over my shoulder down to the creek at the cattails. The shadows were creeping along the creek bank and it looked dark along the shore.

> Late in the day
> When the shadows play
> Long and dark at the water's bank,
> If there you go
> Then you should know
> It lurks deep in the foul and dank.

"I'll get to them after lunch." I had said the words, but I didn't even sound convincing to me.

"There's time enough." She fixed her eyes directly on me like my grandmother would when she had something very important to tell me. "Do you know the full story of Sigaforgas?"

"I've heard that stupid poem." I said trying to sound uninterested.

"The poem came along later. I'm talking about the real story."

My mouth went dry and I couldn't speak a word. I had just about forgotten our earlier conversation. I wondered why she brought it up again.

"Take a sip of tea. Would you like to hear it?"

It was not the type of question meant to be answered. I knew she was going to tell me whether I wanted to hear it or not. I would have left then, but I knew I wouldn't get my two dollars if I left before the job was done.

"This story starts in the late 1700s when this area, still a part of Virginia, was being settled. This was unclaimed country and immigrants were arriving seeking a new life and searching for good land to farm. Among those first immigrant settlers were a Siguer Forgasson and his family.

"In those days, everyone on the farm had chores. The son had to fetch water for the house. Three times a day, at morning, noon, and dusk, he would go down to the creek and fill the large pails with water. It was while doing this one evening he disappeared."

She paused and cocked an eyebrow. "Why, I don't think he was much older than you." She took a sip of tea and continued.

"When he didn't return, Forgasson went to look for him. Darkness was settling in. When he reached the creek, all he found were the pails and the boy's cap. All night and through the next day, he searched up and down the creek. He never found a trace of the boy."

She poured some more tea in her glass. "After that, Forgasson spent each night searching for his lost son. As time went by, he spent less and less time tending the farm and more time prowling the creek bank. The farm went untended and the debts mounted. Soon the farm was lost. His wife, unable to cope, left. Homeless and alone, he lived in the wild along the creek.

"After a while, rumors began to circulate that he was insane and he had really murdered his son and wife. The sheriff of the newly formed Jefferson County soon dispatched a posse to capture the poor man. By this time, he had reverted to living in a mud cave along the banks of the creek, surviving on fish and frogs. He was gaunt and pale, his hair hung in long matted clumps. They placed in the county jail until he could be transferred to an asylum.

"On the day of his transfer, he overpowered the guard and escaped, leaping into a deep ravine. At the bottom, all they found was some blood on the sharp rocks by the waters edge. Many believed he made his way back here. From then on, anytime something unexplained or mysterious happened along Fern Creek, folks would lower their eyes and whisper knowingly, 'Siguer Forgasson.'

"Over time, the true events were forgotten and the legend grew. As the story was told and retold, 'Siguer Forgasson' became the 'Sigaforgas' we now know. In addition, as the name changed, so did the myth grow until 'Sigaforgas' became a monster who lurked along the creek waiting to devour those foolish enough to visit the water's edge after dark."

What does it take
My point to make?
I tell you it's not safe to ignore this.
Know you quite truly
He's mean and unruly
This scourge of the swamp Sigaforgas!

"Well I don't believe it." I blurted out, hoping to convince her and myself.

"I'm sure that's true. Still, there are those who believe that something haunts that creek." She pointed right past my head toward the cattails. "And there seems to have been far too many unexplained disappearances and unfortunate mishaps around here to happen by chance alone."

I couldn't turn around to look. I had the willies. It was just like going in the old well house to reset the pump knowing it was full of spiders. It was like having wasps buzzing around in the shed when you had to go in and get a tool. It was like going into a dark house all alone. It was like things that brush your leg in murky water. Some things just give you the willies. Sometimes, the creek gave me the willies – right at that moment, it gave me the willies. A lot of the time, it gave me the willies. I couldn't figure out why she was talking about this and I didn't like it. I thought my dad and uncle had made that story up to scare us kids. I wondered how she knew about it. I wanted to run home. I couldn't move. How long was I going to have to sit there frozen by the willies?

"Well, its getting late, why don't you go on home and get cleaned up for supper. You can finish up tomorrow," she said letting me off the hook. With that, she folded her napkin and began to clear the table.

"Yes ma'am" I whispered. Finally, I was able to take a breath.

"Put the tools back in the shed before you go."

I walked right up the middle of the road when I crossed the bridge on the way back. I even walked up the hill behind the house to keep from walking along the creek.

That night, I couldn't sleep. The bullfrogs and peepers would drone on and then suddenly fall silent. Occasionally, something would splash in the creek. As I lay between waking and sleep, I imagined Siguer Forgasson scrabbling along the creek so long ago, rooting for food in the muck. I could see him transforming into Sigaforgas, the gill slits forming along his neck, the skin webbing between his fingers, his teeth growing long and pointed. I could see him gliding in the shallows along the banks; hiding in the reeds, pale eyes searching, wet nostrils sniffing. Waiting, always waiting.

I lay motionless in my bed, barely breathing. If I were just quiet enough, if I didn't move, it wouldn't know I was there. It wouldn't creep up the hill from the creek and come to my window. Then the bullfrogs and peepers would start to sing again, chasing away my fears. I could take a deep breath, I could move again.

I was ashamed of being so scared of a silly story, yet I couldn't let go of it. I knew that I would have to face my fear eventually. I still had to clear the cattails for the old woman if I was to get my two dollars. I wondered if she had tried to scare me with the Sigaforgas story so she wouldn't have to pay me. Yeah, maybe that was it! I knew the longer I waited, the harder it would be to gather the courage to go down there.

Just before morning
Please heed my warning
Stay away from the slippery shore.
For there, he who goes
Will be grabbed by the toes
And he'll be gone from here evermore.

Just before dawn, I made up my mind, slipped on jeans and sneakers, quietly opened the screen, and slipped out the window. The moon was still out and I could see the creek just below. The bullfrogs and peepers were singing. Slowly and deliberately, I moved down the hill to the creek. As I approached, the bullfrogs jumped into the water. My heart was in my throat, my pulse pounding in my ears.

I made my way down to a low spot along the bank. There, you could step down to a flat rock as close to the creek as you could get without getting wet. I was just about to step down when I slipped on the dew-covered grass. In the blink of an eye, I landed with a heavy thud on the rock, my face inches from the water.

I sprawled facedown, motionless, startled, the pain pounding in my palms where they struck the rock as I tried to break my fall. The moonlight peeked through the trees above and I could see down in the water. I could smell the fish, the rotting leaves, and the black mud. I could hear the water sluicing through the rocks. I could see movement under the surface. Dark and soft, it swirled around. I strained to look deeper, to see it clearer. The longer I looked, the more I became lost in the swirling, undulating blackness.

How long I lay there staring into the water I couldn't tell. By the time I realized my face was just touching the water and I tried to lift my head, it was too late. Cold, black tendrils had wrapped themselves around my head and neck and were slowly pulling me into the water. I flinched and was immediately sucked down, my head and shoulders fully below the surface. I tried to push back, but my arms sunk in the soft bottom mud up to my elbows. No matter how hard I struggled, I couldn't free myself. I was pulled further and further down into the blackness.

> Know this is true
> It can happen to you
> Even if you're quick as a cat.
> 'Cause before you can think
> You're deep in the drink
> And nothing's left but your hat.

My chest seared in pain and blood thundered hard in my head. Every muscle in my body ached from struggling and lack of oxygen. I was fighting hard against the impulse to open my mouth and inhale. Suddenly, I felt hands grab my shoulders pulling me upward. For a moment, I felt as if I would be torn apart as the as the two opposing forces strained against each other. Finally, I was flung up on the creek bank. I sucked in the sweet night air and let the waves of fear drift away. As the water cleared from my eyes, I could see a figure standing before me.

His face was drawn and pale, so pale that the waning moonlight seemed to seep right through it. His long matted hair hung to his shoulders. He looked straight into me. I started to speak, but he held up a thin hand to stop me. No words were exchanged, but I knew he had wandered here for a long, long time, always searching, never resting, always guarding, – guarding against the thing in the creek. I'll never forget his face so sad, so serious. It told me he would never rest as long as the thing in the creek was there.

The first light of the morning lined the horizon. I watched as he faded away with the mist in the gentle morning breeze. I closed my eyes, and took another deep breath. Whether a second or an hour passed, I'll never know. When I opened my eyes, it was light enough to see I was all alone. I was lying on the bank wet and muddy. I got up and knelt by the running water. It was clear and I could see right to the bottom. Minnows were swimming under the surface searching for their morning meal. I made my way back up the hill to the house, shucked my muddy clothes, and crawled back through the window.

After breakfast, I set out to finish the job I had started and collect my two dollars. When I got to the bridge, I stopped and looked down on the creek and the cattails along the bank of the old woman's yard. All the images from earlier that morning flooded through my head. I couldn't quite put my finger on it, but I knew, that day, I could do whatever I chose along the creek bank and not have to worry. I went straight to the shed, gathered my tools and set about to clear the cattails.

By mid morning, I had cleared the creek bank and stacked everything neatly on the brush pile. I hadn't seen anything of the old woman. I put all the tools back in the shed and went to the back door to collect my money. I knocked, but there was no answer. I peeked in the window, but the house was dark inside. The curtains that had blown through the windows while we had lunch the day before were gone. Leaves and twigs were piled up in the corners

167

of the porch as if it hadn't been swept in a very long time. I tried the door and it opened with a groan. I poked my head inside and looked around. It was empty except for a few dusty newspapers on the floor.

"Hello, is anyone there?" I shouted.

No answer - dark house. I fought back the willies.

I shut the door and looked over to the table where the old woman and I had lunch the day before. It was dusty and bare save for a cattail. I went over to look closer. Tucked under the cattail were two one-dollar bills. I folded them carefully and tucked them in my pocket.

After that, I never saw any sign that anyone lived there. The yard stayed untended. Never saw a car in the drive or a light on in the window. I've never known what became of the old woman.

As to what happened to me that early morning down at the creek bank, your guess is as good as mine; and whether or not you believe in your Sigaforgas is a matter between you and yourself. But, I can tell you this: I still don't like going in the old well house to reset the pump knowing it's full of spiders, having wasps buzzing around in the shed when I'm in there getting a tool, going into a dark house all by myself, or things that brush my leg in murky water.

Now, I spent many happy times down at the creek after that morning. In fact after all these years, I still like to sit on the bank and watch the bluegills swim along in the current. I respect the creek and everything that's in it and I can't really say that I get the willies down there anymore. Never the less, sometimes at dusk when the bullfrogs and peepers suddenly fall silent, I head on back up the hill.

Then all they can do
For what's left of you

Is sing the sad funeral chorus.
So, that's all I'll say
Wish you well on your way
And pray you don't meet Sigaforgas!

EXILED[13]

Tamara's tears had dried by the time she poured half of her large cup of Quik Cola down the sink, replacing it with a half pint of cheap vodka. *This should make it easier.* She downed almost a third in a single gulp, then climbed into the tub. Warm water rose to her chin as she slid down. Grime and mold lurked in the seam where the wall met the porcelain. *When was the last time the housemaid cleaned this? What does it matter?* She drank down another third of her vodka-cola, waiting for her stomach to accept it before taking a breath. The box cutter, taken from her husband's workbench, lay in the soap dish. The tip of the blade was broken. *Should have changed it. Would have made a cleaner cut.* Alcohol coursed through her body. *Soon.*

Noise seeped through the wall. People noise, raised voices. Nothing distinguishable, maybe Spanish, maybe not. The alcohol was now in full control of her head. *Better finish up.* She sucked down the remaining vodka-cola, letting the cup fall to the floor. The noise grew less distinguishable. *Wait just a bit more for the vodka to do its job.* She watched the faucet drip until her eyes couldn't stay focused. *Get the knife and do it. Quickly.* She reached out. *Do it before you pass out. Do it!* She grabbed the box cutter and raked it across her wrist.

Red tendrils of blood swirled out into the water as she was whisked down into the whirlpool of her alcohol induced dreams. Images floated in and out from the black confines of her mind.

***

---

[13] "Exiled" appeared in *Through My Eyes,* An anthology published by Fantasia Divinity Magazine, 9/2017.

...The garbled intercom blared at her. *Why am I here?* The hallways were empty. The classrooms were empty. No one was to be found in the office. *My children! I'm here for them.* Tamara ran through the deserted building calling for them, but no reply came. She followed the drops of blood that spattered the white tile floors, each leading to an empty room...

... Her mother writhed on a gurney as it rolled lazily down a sterile white corridor. *Where are they taking her?* Tamara ran behind, her feet slipping on the polished red tile floor. The harder she ran, the deeper her feet sank into the shiny red surface. The thick, coagulating blood, sucked her down...

...Her husband ran up the stairs from his workshop in the basement. He lunged, slashing at her with his box cutter. *Why are you doing this?* She held up her hands to fend him off. Searing pain stabbed her wrists. Blood spewed from the gaping wounds...

...She ambled through a dark concourse. She had the sense that unfriendly, hungry things lingered in the deepest shadows along indistinct walls. *Where am I? Why are they reaching out for me?* As she moved forward, the space around her narrowed. Ahead, she saw a glimmer of light. *An opening!. I must reach it.* She felt the hungry things' boney hands touching her, ever so lightly, ever so inquisitively. *Go! Now, before they take me. Go!* Just as she reached the opening, a revenant raised up directly in front of her. She looked into its pale eyes. They held only despair. The light was just beyond. *If I could only reach it!* The revenant bolted straight ahead. Her soul withered under the blast of frigid desolation as it passed...

***

Tamara opened her eyes, glad to be awake. Her night had turned out to be an endless loop of troubling dreams. She realized she was lying on a freshly made bed. The door to her room was open and the curtains were pulled back. She knew it was light

172

outside, but darkness surrounded her. Everything was cast in the grey pallor of dusk . It was unusually quiet. *Something's not right. Why is my room open, why is the bed made up? Why am I here?* She stood, just as the housemaid entered with an armful of bath towels.

"What's going on here?" Tamara called out, stepping forward toward the young woman. The housemaid continued moving toward the bath. "Listen to me!" she shouted, grabbing the housemaid's forearm. As her hand reached the young woman's arm, brilliant sunlight flooded Tamara's senses. Vibrant colors replaced the gray pallet. The robin's egg blue of the housemaid's uniform shimmered and the deep red of the roses in the floral wallpaper pulsed. Sounds assaulted her ears. The morning traffic roared while a TV broadcast from the room next door flowed through the wall. The odor of starched laundry, mixed with the scents of musky perfume and pine cleaner filled her head. She quickly withdrew her hand and everything sank back into twilight and silence. *What's happening?*

The young woman gave no acknowledgement. Tamara moved directly in front of the woman. She held up her hands to stop her and force a response. The woman did not flinch. She did not stop. Once again, the dreary twilight evaporated as the woman reached Tamara's hands. She passed through Tamara like a warm breeze blows through a lake house on a summer's afternoon.

Instantly, Tamara knew all there was to know about the woman. She was twenty three, sixth child of a migrant. At age six, she fell from a truck, breaking her arm. For want of medical treatment, it never healed properly. Raped at thirteen by a neighbor, she never told anyone because he threatened to tell the INS her father was an illegal. After earning her nursing degree, she will marry her beautiful fireman. She carries his child. Most of all,

Tamara sensed the woman's hope and belief that her life would be happy despite her painful past.

Then, she was gone and the twilight dullness returned. Tamara looked into the mirror hanging over the dented chest of drawers. She saw a pale, desolate caricature of herself. It reminded her of the revenant in her dream.

Panic seized Tamara. *I must get home to my family. I've got to tell them how much I love them. I've got to tell them how this is was all a horrible mistake.* She looked around the room for her suitcase. It was gone. She went to the closet to retrieve her clothes but it was empty. She rushed out to the parking lot to find her car was missing as well.

She stood for some time on the crumbling sidewalk outside the dingy motel, watching the business of the ordinary world go on silently in the dim twilight. *What's going on?* People trudged up and down the sidewalk while cars arrived and departed from the parking lot shared with the liquor store. At first, Tamara called out to every person she saw. Not one of them so much as looked in her direction. *Can't anyone hear me?* She even tried standing in front of a few. Just like the housemaid, each passed through her. Every time, she was instantly imbued with their memories and emotions. Some were happy, some sad. Most were content with their lives. Once, she stepped in the path of an oncoming car. It passed through her without any noticeable effect.

In her twilight world, Tamara had no sense of time; but the clock on the bank across the street marked the hours as the day wound down. *I must get home. Maybe all I need is to make contact with someone I know. Everything will be OK if I can get to my family. That's all it will take.*

Home was only a couple of miles down the road. The day still had several hours of sunlight left and she felt it would be better to arrive before it got dark. She was careful to avoid contact with people, not wanting to take on any new memories or emotions. Soon, she turned onto her street.

Her car was in the driveway. *How did that get here?* As she got closer, she could see her husband on the porch watching the girls play. She called out, waving her hand. No one looked. She broke into a run up the sidewalk, calling to them. No response. *Can't they hear me? Why aren't they looking for me? Am I so meaningless to them they haven't noticed I was gone? Do they just not care?*

***

The new Tamara put the finishing touches on the pot roast and looked out the window. She saw the revenant standing at the front gate. She knew sooner or later that it would show up in desperation. She put a large bowl of potatoes on the table, then joined her husband on the front porch.

"Time for supper. Lauren, you and Leslie go set the table," she said, as she gathered her husband in her arms and gave him a kiss. "Jerry, go on, I'll be there in a minute." She waited until they were inside to step down from the porch and walk out to the front gate to meet the revenant.

"I knew you would come back. Every exile does," she said calmly. "At first, I tried to go back. I can tell you it's quite impossible. I know this will be painful for you to accept, but this life is no longer yours. You lost it when you gave up last night. You are a revenant now - an exile. I was like you. I too had given up. That's when my life was captured. Exiles seek out the weak and vulnerable who have given up on lives that can still be fulfilled. They capture those lives just as theirs were captured and leave the revenant exiled, wandering in the shadows. I wandered a long time before I found you."

"Did I die?"

"No, but you wanted to and that's all that mattered. You wanted to die. You tried to die. You had given in to despair. That was all the opening I needed. It only took a small push, then you were out. I took your place. Now you are a revenant, exiled. Don't waste your time here. You can't come back. Once you accept that, you can start looking. Hang around bus stations and seedy apartment buildings. Old motels are good hunting grounds too. Don't waste time following happy people and stay away from dopers and drunks."

She turned and walked up the steps and through the front door. She looked back out through the living room window. An evening breeze rolled down the street, sweeping the leaves and the revenant out of sight.

FOR DREAM, INSERT CARD[14]

It was the strangest thing she had ever seen, with tubes and wires protruding haphazardly from the bright blue orb that sat on the nightstand. It appeared to be some Japanese electronic gadget, resembling a cross between a gumball dispenser and a cappuccino machine on steroids. Closer scrutiny revealed what were no doubt instructions in many languages. Larraine perused the list until she found a single sentence in English: For dream, insert card. A large red arrow pointed to a nondescript slot just above an electronic display that read:

$1 US
FOR ASSISTANCE, DIAL 666 223 5825

So far, the trip had been a huge calamity. This was to have been her last, grand adventure before tying the knot. Larraine thought it would bring her life into focus. It had only been a major disappointment. She had missed her booked flight. Damn. She didn't know passports even had an expiration date. That took a week of her allotted three to straighten out. When she had finally arrived, her reservation at the beach-front resort had been cancelled. She ended up in a crumbling, old castle that had been used as a prison before its reincarnation as a cheap hotel. Surrounded by disintegrating hovels, it sat high on the hill above the resort, far away from the luxury of the beach. Larraine had a sink and commode in the tiny room, but the showers were located at the end of the tier. Her stomach had been queasy for the first

---

[14] For Dream Insert Card was accepted for publication online in *This Dark Matter*, 2/2015, and appeared on line in *CommuterLit* 10/2016.

week of her stay, and she had spent most of her time counting the tiles around the commode in her room.

Larraine had so desperately wanted an adventure that she was willing to try almost anything to salvage the remaining time before returning home. She SO did not want to be here, especially when it was one of those days when everything seemed to go wrong. She didn't want to be here, but she didn't want to go home either. This was supposed to be her big adventure. So far, it had been a disaster. Returning home wouldn't be any better. It wasn't going to be easy, but somehow she had to confront her mother. She would have to listen to the "I told you so" routine. Her mother had been dead set against the trip all along. "Larraine, what'll you find there that you don't already have here? Freddy is a nice boy. He'll be assistant manager at the Sizzler in no time. Nice girls don't take vacations alone."

Given the prospects, what did she have to lose? Her hand trembled as she punched the number into the phone. After a series of beeps and tones, an operator with a thick, Oriental accent answered.

"Hello, this is Dora, how I help you?'

"Yes, I am calling about your machine. What does it do?"

"Oh yes, put credit card in."

"I can see that, but what does it do?"

"Put credit card in, you get dream."

"What kind of dream?"

"Yes, put credit card in, you get dream." The phone clicked and the dial tone returned.

"Yes, what do I have to lose?" she said to the dial tone as she placed the handset back in its cradle. She reached across the bed and retrieved her purse. Deep in the bottom, she found her wallet and fished out her credit card. She looked it over while she pondered whether or not to take a chance. She glanced over to the blue orb. She swore that for an instant, the display read:

WHAT YOU GOT TO LOSE, LARAINE?

She blinked and looked at the display again. This time it read:

$1 US
FOR ASSISTANCE, DIAL 666 223 5825

Larraine awkwardly worked the card into the slot.

She watched his lithe body saunter away. *Watch out, remember you're engaged.* She had been sunning herself along the beach when the young man had come along. He was an Adonis. Their conversation started with a simple, "Hello, my name is Andreas." They had chatted while the sun marched across the afternoon sky. They sipped tall, cool, Limoncello cocktails and walked along the beach. They agreed to meet for dinner and then dancing. Colors swooped and swirled behind her closed eyelids as the music soared, taking her back to sun, sand, and sea - total relaxation. So why couldn't she let go? This is what she had wished for - an adventure, a real adventure. Larraine longed for a night of romance, a week of passion. She was weary of discount matinees with Freddy and his awkward groping on the couch. She wanted so much to give way to her desires, to make love with Andreas on the beach beneath the stars while the waves crashed upon the shore.

Larraine awoke to the irritating buzz of the phone next to her bed. She had arranged for a wake-up call each morning at 7:00 AM so she could get into the shower before her fellow touristas. The dream last night had seemed so real. *But it was just a dream, right?* She looked at the blue orb on the nightstand. Her credit card protruded from the slot. The display read:

DREAM COMPLETED
YOUR CARD CHARGED $1 US
THANK YOU

She pulled the credit card out of the slot and the display blinked:

TO CONTINUE, INSERT CARD - $10 US
FOR ASSISTANCE DIAL 666 223 5825

So that's their game. See if they get ten bucks from me! Still, she was quite frustrated that the alarm had awakened her just as Andreas was taking her in his arms. Although her mind told her it had all been a dream, her body was still flush with excitement unfulfilled. She looked at the display again:

WHY NOT TREAT YOUSELF?

She picked up the phone and punched in the numbers.

"Hello Miss Larraine, this is Dora, how I help you?'

"Dora, I am calling about your machine. If I put my credit card in, will my dream continue?"

"Oh yes, put credit card in."

"I can see that, but will my dream pick up where it left off?"

"Put credit card in, you get dream."

"But will it be my dream?"

"Yes, put credit card in, you get dream." The phone clicked and the dial tone returned. Larraine stared at the blue orb. It's only ten bucks, she thought. She reached over, tingling with anticipation and guided her card back into the slot.

The sun was soft and the boat rocked gently. It wasn't so bad running out of fuel, until Larraine realized they might drift out to sea. She could just make out the windows high in the castle wall. Her window was one of those on the third floor. She wondered if anyone was looking or if anyone could see them, or if anyone cared. She lay on the sundeck. Champaign cooled in the carafe. Andreas's hands were strong and soothing as he rubbed her bare back with tanning lotion. He had worked his way to the small of her back when he stopped. She exhaled in mild exasperation. He stood up and peered toward the shore. Silhouetted against the brilliant blue sky, he looked like a bronze statue. She rolled on her back in anticipation that his hands would find more to anoint.

"We drift too far," he said.

"Won't the tide take us back in?"

"No, I must try to swim to shore for help. Go to the cabin and find the flare gun. If I do not make it back in 2 hours, fire it off." He ran to the side of the boat and dove headlong into the clear water. Larraine watched as he swam away from the boat. He had gone about 100 yards when she saw the first dark fin. In an instant, it was joined by two more knifing through the water. She called out to Andreas. As he turned, he yelled, "Larraine, get the gun, quickly, get the gun." Just before she turned back to the cabin, she saw the fins swirl in a tight circle around Andreas.

Larraine awoke to the gentle rocking motion of the boat. On a small table next to the bunk sat the blue orb. The display read:

DREAM COMPLETED
YOUR CARD CHARGED $10 US
WHAT?

I must still be dreaming, she thought. She jumped up and ran to the deck. The sun was low in the sky. She peered in every direction, but there was no sign of Andreas. Even worse, there was

181

no sign of land. She rushed back into the cabin, frantically searching for the gun. Every compartment was empty. She clambered on deck to find everything gone. Not even the carafe and champagne were to be found. She returned to the cabin. The compartments, bunks and chairs were now missing. The only thing she saw, other than the hull, was the table with the blue orb sitting on it. She pulled the credit card out of the slot and the display blinked:

TO CONTINUE, INSERT CARD - $100 US
YOU KNOW REST

The deck above began to dissolve. Not knowing what else to do, Larraine shoved the credit card back into the slot.

The storm whipped the trees outside and she huddled into her quilt. The building shook, lurching and jumping, and the little china horse fell off the mantel. She knelt on the tile floor, carefully picking up the shards of glass. *Why this one?* Larraine examined the fragments in the dim candle light. She could not hold back her tears as she cradled the pieces in her hands. It was the one Freddy had bought her back before she had run off on the ill-conceived adventure to discover herself. She had broken Freddy's heart when she returned with Andreas. It wasn't until later that she would find out Andreas had married her only to gain entrance to the US. He now spent his evenings drinking and womanizing, while she sat weeping, wishing that she had never gone on the ill-fated trip, wishing she had married Freddy instead. Shadows quivered on the wall as the candle flickered, then fizzled to nothing. She ducked as the plate smashed against the wall behind her. Andreas had returned, drunk again. He lunged for her, but fell over a chair as she ran to the bedroom.

The blue orb sat on the chest of drawers. Larraine glared at the display.

DREAM COMPLETED
YOUR CARD CHARGED $100 US
BETTER TRY AGAIN

She snatched the card from the slot. Immediately the display changed:

TO CONTINUE, INSERT CARD - $1000 US
NO FOOL AROUND, LARRAINE

She roughly jammed the card back in.

The chattering birds made her smile, until she heard a growl. She looked up toward the house. Fierce eyes flashed in the gloom behind the window. The prickles on her neck told her she was being watched. Larraine hid in the bushes at the side of the house while Andreas thrashed about inside. This was her chance to escape. During his transformation, there was a brief window of opportunity in which she hoped to make her getaway. The back door crashed open. Andreas, in mid-transformation, tumbled down the steps and sprawled in a grotesque heap. Barely recognizable as the handsome young man she had so foolishly married after a lust-filled week, he writhed in the dirt as the hair grew on his misshapen limbs and fangs shot out through foaming lips. Her only hope was to make a dash for the car. If she could only get inside and lock the doors, she might have a chance. Andreas lay between her and the garage. She braced herself, then sprang forward down the path. Ten strides and she leapt over Andreas. His eyes, filled with rage, followed her as she landed in full stride beyond his grasp and disappeared into the garage. Larraine slammed the door shut and threw the bolt. As she turned around, her heart sank. No car.

She dropped to her knees before the blue orb. Her tears formed tiny globs of mud as they fell onto the dusty, earthen floor. She wiped her eyes with the back of her hand as she looked at the display:

DREAM COMPLETED
YOUR CARD CHARGED $1000 US
CONGRATULATIONS
YOU WIN FREE DREAM

Larraine yanked the card from the slot. The display flashed a new message:

TO CONTINUE, INSERT CARD - NO CHARGE
HURRY, LARRAINE

With trembling fingers, she held the card above the slot. She placed it at the opening, but it would not go in. She tried again. Still, the opening would not accept the card. Raising up, she brought the weight of her body down on the card, forcing it roughly into the slot, edges grinding in resistance until it finally disappeared into the machine.

She slammed forward as the brakes screeched and the car skidded to an abrupt stop. Larraine looked at the letter that had flown off the seat and now lay on the dirty floorboard. She looked in the rearview mirror. No sign of the beast thing. She loosened her seat belt so she could retrieve the letter, then flung open the door and ran across the street. She hesitated at the post box, not knowing if she should really send the letter. It seemed foolish, but she wanted to apologize to Freddy. One act of contrition for the harm she had done to him. All she had to do was drop the letter in the chute, get in the car, and drive until the nightmare was far behind her. She watched the letter disappear into the dark recesses of the post box. Suddenly, she heard a wrenching scream and the sound of shattering glass. Larraine looked back to her car and gasped. The beast thing was pounding car windows with its club-like fists, sending shards of glass flying. It ripped the door off its hinges and stuck its grotesque head inside, letting out a howl of rage. Larraine spied a narrow opening between the buildings and quickly slipped around the corner. The lane was night-dark, even at noon. Through the gloom, she could see this was a dead-end. Trapped. A rat in a maze, a tiger in a cage, every cliché she could think of - she was trapped. She tore through the alley, ducked into a doorway, and tried to squeeze into nothingness. The beast thing appeared at the alley's opening, a black silhouette against the sunlit street behind. It raised its misshapen head and sniffed the air. Dropping to all fours, it began to creep toward her.

Larraine gave the door a last, mighty shove. It swung open freely and she tumbled into nothingness. She was surrounded by grey. It was like standing at the end of a boat dock in a heavy fog. She reached out, searching for something, anything with her hands. She felt nothing but the smooth, cold floor. She strained her eyes to make out any shape as she got to her feet. Nothing. The silence was pierced by a loud banging sound. Larraine whirled around and spied the door. It seemed suspended in the gray. She could not see a wall or any other feature, only the door. Another loud crash rang out followed by a long, gruesome howl. A steady tattoo of blasts followed, accompanied by the beast's feral screams. With each battering, Larraine could hear the door creak and crack. It would not be long until the door crumbled under the assault. She turned, determined to run as far into the gray as her shaking legs would take her.

The blue orb sat directly in front of her. The gray closed in, suffocating her senses. She heard the door crash to the ground somewhere behind her. Larraine's legs, no longer able to hold her up, buckled and she fell to the ground, face inches from the display:

DREAM COMPLETED
NO CHARGE

The orb spit her credit card out and it fluttered to the ground. The display blinked:

TO CONTINUE, INSERT CARD - $10,000 US
YOUR ASS IN BIG TROUBLE

She stared at the credit card, numbers blurring in front of her eyes, wondering if ...

A GAME OF TAG[15]

I remember that house, perched up there on the creek bank. The third window from the left, low to the ground, was my room. We had no air conditioning then. On hot summer nights, a rusty screen that could hardly resist the thumps of moths was all that kept what lurked outside from coming in. My bed lay under the window to catch the occasional breeze. The curtains would draw in and then press out against the screen as if the whole house was taking a deep breath.

I remember the night noises along the creek bank. Katydids, loud and raucous, joined the chirping of crickets to fill the darkness with a plaintive ballad. The deep baritone calls of bullfrogs rolled up the steep bank. The soft, splitting sound of the creek, as it flowed around the huge pock-marked boulder which sat defiantly in its path, floated through the heavy air. This discordant symphony would coalesce into a driving rhythm, as if the night was suddenly frightened: making its heart beat wildly. Then, as quickly as the crescendo reached its apex, all fell silent at the sound of a breaking twig, the rustle of dead leaves, or an unfamiliar splash in the creek's murky water.

I remember waiting in the silence: waiting for it to come up to my window. I knew it lurked in the dark, muddy water in a hole beneath that rock. I knew it subsisted on the cold-blooded creatures that slithered in the mud on the creek bottom. I also knew it hungered in the dark for the warm, soft flesh of children.

Slowly, silently, it would make its way up the bank under the cover of the sounds of the night, stopping only when the symphony was interrupted. I waited. If I were completely still,

---

[15] "A Game Of Tag" appeared in *Brief Grislys - An Anthology of Horror Stories of 1000 Words or Less* published by Apochrophyle Press 2013.

completely silent, it couldn't find me. If I moved or made a sound, I knew it would tear through the flimsy screen and rip my body apart; stuffing the bloody pulp into its gaping maw, licking the gore from its bony claws.

I remember lying there in the stifling heat night after night, drawing the covers up over my head, not moving. It couldn't smell me, it couldn't see me if I had the covers pulled over my head. Each breath was measured, taking an eternity, so that the movement of my chest could not be detected. It was like diving down to the bottom of the pool and holding your breath until your lungs almost burst trying to swim to the top; but on these endless summer nights, I had to stay perfectly still. On the hottest nights, the sweat trickled along my neck but still I couldn't move. My lungs would ache for just one, long, cool draft of air, but I didn't dare pull the covers down. Not while it lurked outside. I lay completely still, no movement to give me away.

Some nights I couldn't tell where it lurked, but I kept my covers pulled up tight. Other nights I knew it was crouching right outside my window. Those nights I wanted to leap out of the bed to run and hide, but I knew it would be too quick. I knew it would catch me. Through those terrifying summer nights, we played this cat-and-mouse game.

I remember the night I awoke to silence. A cool breeze drifted over me and the soft fresh night air filled my lungs. I had only a single moment to enjoy it before I realized in horror that I had kicked the covers off and left myself exposed. It was then that I felt the drop of water fall on my face.

I looked up into its pale eyes, looming only inches from my face.   One cold, wet

hand slammed down hard on my chest pinning me to the bed, while the other grasped my head pushing it down into my pillow. I wanted to scream out for help; but my heart, filled with terror, pounded my throat closed and beat the air from my lungs. Large, flat, eyes drifted closer to my face. A dank breath poured down, stinging my cheeks like an icy blast on a winter's day.

As those weeping eyes drew close, I saw the universe of black desolation within.

I remember the pain, like the time I burned my hand on the stove, but everywhere in my body and all at once. Then blackness, stillness.

I opened my eyes to see a child in bed. I was holding it down with ruthless hands. Drawing back, I gazed at the oddly familiar face. I shivered in the cloying night air. That child was me! I retched with the sudden and overwhelming realization that my body had been taken. I stood there for a long time, confused and terrified. I wanted my body back, but I knew it no longer belonged to me. Then, the sleeping child that had been me pulled the covers up. A smile, like the taunting smirk of a child having just tagged a playmate "It", spread across his beaming face.

Resigned to my fate, I slipped out of the window and back down to the creek where I found a hole under the rock.

That was many years ago. Since then, I have dined on the cold flesh of the small beasts that slither on the bottom of the creek. I have waited here in the cold and murky water.

I remember. I will keep an eye on that house. Someday, a child will sleep in that room again. I will , and when the katydids and crickets sing on a summer's night, I will creep up to that window and if that child is not careful, I will have a warm bed to sleep in once again.

ABOUT THE AUTHOR

Paul Stansbury is a life long native of Kentucky. Now retired, he lives in Danville, Kentucky. He is the owner of Sheppard Press. He is the author of *Inversion - Not Your Ordinary Stories, Inversion II - Creatures, Fairies, and Haints, Oh My!*, and *Down By the Creek – Ripples and Reflections*, all published by Sheppard Press. His novelette, *Little Green Men?* was published by The Society of Misfit Stories.

His stories appearing in print/ebook anthologies:

- "A Game Of Tag" and "Dark Meat" appeared in Brief Grislys published by Apocryphile Press
- "Sigaforgas" appeared in Neo-Legends To Last A Deathtime published by KY Story
- "The Ghost Eye" appeared in Frightening published by SEZ Publishing
- "Takers" appeared in Out of the Cave published by MacKenzie Publishing
- "Phantasmal" appeared in In Media Res, Stories From the In-Between published by Writespace Houston
- "Under the Wolf Moon" appeared in Nocturnal Natures published by Zimbell House Publishing
- "Spirit Painter" appeared in Book 3: 30 Authors-30 Stories published by Flash Fiction Magazine
- "Exiled" appeared in See Through My Eyes: A Ghost Mystery Anthology published by Fantasia Divinity Magazine
- "Selkie Cove" appeared in Mirrors & Thorns - An OWS Ink Dark Fairy Tale Anthology published by Catterfly Publishing (A Division of OWS Ink. LLC)
- "Little Green Men?" appeared in The Society of Misfit Stories Presents...Volume One published by Bards and Sages Publishing

- "The Girl In The Harvest Moon" appeared in Autumn's Harvest: An Autumn Fantasy Anthology published by Fantasia Divinity Magazine
- "Mulded" appeared in Anthology Askew 006 published by Rhetoric Askew
- "The Scroll And The Silver Kazoo" appeared in The Rabbit Hole, Weird Tales Volume 1 published by The Writers Co-op

His poetry has appeared in The Rising Phoenix Review, Young Ravens Literary Review, Strange Poetry and Kentucky Monthly and read as part of a concert by Sounding Joy: A Woman's Life.

He is a contributing writer for the Danville Advocate Messenger Newspaper, Scheduling Coordinator for The Jeanne Penn Lane Celebration of Kentucky Writers (Formerly Historic Penn's Store Kentucky Writers Day Celebration), and a member of the Board of Directors of Scarlet Cup Theater.

Paul Stansbury
www.paulstansbury.com
www.facebook.com/paulstansbury

BOOKS FROM SHEPPARD PRESS

Down By The Creek – Ripples and Reflections by Paul Stansbury
ISBN 978-0-9986516-0-6 paperback
ISBN 978-0-9986516-1-3 e-book

Inversion – Not Your Ordinary Stories by Paul Stansbury
ISBN 978-0-9986516-3-7 paperback
ISBN 978-0-9986516-4-4 e-book

Inversion II – Creatures, Fairies, and Haints, Oh My! by Paul
Stansbury
ISBN 978-0-9986516-5-1 paperback
ISBN 978-0-9986516-6-8 e-book

*By George – A Collection Of Childhood Experiences and
Anecdotes* by George Herbert Stansbury, Jr.
ISBN 978-0-9986516-2-0 paperback

Migrant Times and Other Musings by George Boursaw
Available only at Lulu - https://www.lulu.com

Printing done by Lulu.com